RIVALS

AN ENEMIES TO LOVERS MAFIA ROMANCE

MAFIA ELITE, BOOK 7

AMY MCKINLEY

ARROWSCOPE PRESS, LLC

Rivals

Copyright © 2022 Amy McKinley

All rights reserved. Without limiting the rights under copyright reserved above, no part of this publication may be reproduced, stored, in or introduced into retrieval system, or transmitted, in any form, or by any means (electronic mechanical, photocopying, recording, or otherwise) without the prior written permission of both the copyright owner and the above publisher of this book.

This book is a work of fiction. Names, characters, places, brands, media, and incidents are either the products of the author's imagination or are used fictitiously. The author acknowledges the trademarked status and trademark owners of various products referenced in this work of fiction, which have been used without permission. The publication/use of these trademarks is not authorized, associated with, or sponsored by the trademark owners.

(p) ISBN-13: 978-1-951919-32-0

(e) ISBN-13: 978-1-951919-31-3

Publisher: Arrowscope Press, LLC; www.arrowscopepress.com

Editing— Kate Birdsall, Line Editor, Taylor Anhalt, Proofreader, Red Adept Editing

Cover Design—T.E. Black Designs; www.teblackdesigns.com

Author photo provided by—Brookelyn Anhalt of lovely.life.photography; https://www.facebook.com/LovelyLifePhotography-102253596490708

Interior Formatting & Design— Arrowscope Press, LLC; www.arrowscope-press.com

THE FAMILY

**Chicago Outfit
Italian American Mafia**

<u>Caruso Family</u>

Maximus "Max" (boss, married Liliana Brambilla)
Elena (sister, married Marco La Rosa)
Tony (Max's half-brother)
Parents/former boss
Antonio – (father, former boss, deceased)
Maria (first wife to Antonio, deceased, Max's Mom)
Nicole (second wife to Antonio)
Vito (advisor to boss)
Maria's family from Italy
Salvio "Sal" (cousin)
Cristiano (cousin)
Tommasso (cousin)
Aunt Rosa (lives in Sicily)

Brambilla Family

Luca "Luc" (boss, married Summer)
Liliana "Lil" (half-sister, married Max Caruso)
Sal (underboss, cousin)
Dino (advisor to boss)
Eva (cousin, deceased)
Parents/former boss
Benito (former boss, deceased)
Julia (Benito's wife, deceased)
Vincenzo (Julia's Sicilian father, Liliana's grandfather)

La Rosa Family

Marco (boss, married Elena Caruso)
Nico (underboss, brother, engaged to Hailey)
Trey (brother)
Sofia (sister, married Enzo Vitale)
Maso (Robert's brother, advisor)
Tom (captain)
Parents/former boss
Robert (former boss)
Angela (Robert's wife)

Vitale Family

Enzo (boss, married Sofia La Rosa)
Emiliana "Em" (sister, married Stefano Rossi)
Aldo (advisor to boss)
Renato "Ren" (captain)
Parents/former boss
Emilio (former boss)
Alessia (Emilio's wife)

Rossi Family

Stefano (boss, married Emiliana Vitale)
Camila (sister, married Vic Pavlov)
Alfonso (brother, deceased)
Marissa (sister, deceased)
Drago (advisor to the boss)
Parents/former boss
Frank (father, former boss, deceased)
Carla (Frank's wife, deceased)

Russian Mafia
Pavlov Bratva

Pavlov Bratva

Yuri (boss)
Mischa (wife)
Ivan (eldest son, former underboss, deceased)
Victor "Vic" (son, underboss, married Camila Rossi)
Katya (angel of death, assassin)

New York Outfit
Italian American Mafia

Amato Family

Leo (boss)
Guido (son, underboss)
Ben (cousin, soldier, deceased)

Tucci Family

Joey (boss)
Linda (2nd wife)
Ricco (step-son, underboss, Linda's son)
Mia (daughter)

Verretti Family

Dante (boss)
Calvino "Cal" (brother, underboss)
Adriano (youngest brother, assassin)

CHAPTER ONE

MIA

I felt the change in the air and in my bones as I gripped the doorknob, preparing to face whatever trap my stepbrother had set for me that day.

I had work to do, but I couldn't stay. Things were too dangerous, especially if Ricco and my father discovered that the problems cropping up with the sex-trafficking ring they ran—the broken-down trucks and missing girls—were because of me.

I'm the rat. To be caught would have been a fate worse than death. Since my existence sometimes bordered on that, anyway, I had to listen to my gut. It was screaming to leave.

Slipping out of my bedroom, I measured each breath as my heels clicked on the wood floor and I neared the stairway that would lead me closer to my escape. I would leave with the clothes on my back, a stockpile of weapons strategically strapped to my body, and Mom's elegant gold-bar necklace with the miniature chamomile flower etched in the base, which I never left home without.

For the fifteen years since she'd died, I'd been playing an elaborate chess game with my father, Ricco, and my life. But over the past few months, things had escalated. I wouldn't have put anything past Ricco, and that morning was no different. It was a game of cat and mouse, and I damn well would not be the mouse in the end.

I crept along the hallway until I was two steps from the second-floor landing when the click of a door opening shattered my focus. Pure evil permeated the air, causing the fine hairs all over my body to rise. The familiar cloying scent of my stepbrother's strong cologne announced his presence, and I tensed to run.

A punishing grip closed around my upper arm, jerking my body back, and I lost my footing, falling into the hallway table and vase. Glass shattered in a crash across the floor. I fell into the shards of glass, pain piercing my hip as I felt something sharp tear through my skin.

I pushed off the ground, ignoring the blood that trickled down my leg from the gash. He grabbed me again and jerked. I stiffened, refusing to fall into him. A pinch in my upper arm had me craning my neck and looking over my shoulder to see what he'd done.

Ricco grinned at me. He'd stabbed me with a needle.

Freezing liquid raced up my arm as his hand clamped over my mouth. I struggled, kicking back, but his hand only tightened as he waited for the drug to work. Within minutes, I felt the foreign substance take effect, infecting my blood and making my movements languid. I met the eyes of my tormentor before I lost the ability to fight.

"Hello, sis." Dark intent churned within his obsidian gaze, and a malicious smirk grazed his face. I should have experienced a surge of adrenaline. I didn't. The drug's effects were swift, and my body was no longer my own to control.

He hefted me over a broad shoulder, and my arms flopped by the side of my head. My thoughts were sluggish, but I tried to pay attention as he turned and went in the opposite direction from where I'd been headed. With each step, the effort to keep my eyes open became too great. Not even the fear of where he was taking me or what it meant for my future could stop the darkness from descending.

Time blinked in and out, creating a slideshow of still images: the hallway, the back seat of a black sedan, arctic-gray cement floors, and a row of windowless, locked doors. Finally, a white ceiling remained as a fixed viewpoint for what seemed like—and probably was—hours. *How long have I been in here?* Without my phone, or any sort of clock, I couldn't tell how much time had passed since Ricco had tossed me on this lumpy cot.

A tsunami of dread rose, and I balanced precariously on the crest of the giant wave as I became more aware of my surroundings. Sensation returned in increments, starting with my fingers and toes.

A stuttered influx of adrenaline fired through me as the tan steel door opened, and my stepbrother walked into the room. His dark shoulder-length hair was slicked back in his signature ponytail. My gaze dropped to the deep indentation in his chin, where he had trouble shaving the whiskers that grew within, so he wore a perpetual five o'clock shadow. It didn't matter—that spot was still noticeable and a chink in his armor, something I used to tease him about unmercifully when we were teenagers. I called him "Buttface" and told him his chin reminded me of a hairy butthole. It was mean, but he did worse things.

I snapped my attention back to him, working hard to focus on what he was saying. My lips tingled as feeling returned to them, and I fought from grimacing. There was no point in letting him know how much of the drug had worn off.

He glanced at his watch, a ten-thousand-dollar monstrosity of gold and diamonds. "Our father has decided to marry you to that politician."

Not your *father, asshole*. It was a wasted thought because Dad sure as hell preferred Ricco. Not only that, but he would hand over the reins to the family legacy to him, the boy he took in after the death of the captain of our guard, Ricco's birth father.

The conversation I'd overheard the night before between my dad and stepbrother about marriage wreaked havoc in my mind as I considered who I might be paired with and how my father would benefit.

The Verretti boss was out. Dante had declined my father's proposition for an arrangement between our families, including my marrying either of his two brothers. Since they were no longer candidates, my father pivoted in another direction—a very powerful and well-connected politician. I did not want that life. Nor would I be safe. There was only one way I would be protected, and I needed to figure out how to achieve that.

I'd edged closer to the office door the night before to better hear the fate of my future. But when Ricco threw his name into the pot, I'd made myself scarce. He was a snake, and I wouldn't have put it past him to go behind my father's back to benefit his position in the family. Each day was much of the same as I eased myself closer to being trapped with a man I wouldn't choose.

I needed a plan.

Ricco's upper lip curled, and I forced myself to listen to the venom he was spewing. "We have enough people in our pocket in government positions. Your marriage to one of them would be a wasted opportunity."

I held my breath. Whatever was coming, it wouldn't be good.

"What we need is an ally, and Guido is very interested in providing that through his marriage to you."

I gave up part of the farce and voiced how ignorant Ricco was. "Guido Amato isn't an underboss anymore. His position was stripped from him by his stupidity." The son and former underboss of one of New York's Mafia families wasn't someone I'd ever liked. And his recent stunt had cost him his position in the family. Messing with the Five Families was asinine, and Guido had been lucky to escape with his life.

My foot dangled off the mattress, and Ricco tapped it with his, watching closely for a physical response to see if the drug had worn all the way off. When none came, I knew it bought me a little time, and I had to use every second.

"In a few short weeks, Guido will be boss of his family with his new wife by his side—you."

I snorted because the only way that would happen was if he murdered his father. After the stunt he'd pulled trying to get to Summer, whom the Chicago Mafia had protected, I doubted his ability to infiltrate any rank close enough to the Amato boss to fulfill that goal.

"And as a bonus," Ricco continued, ignoring my derision, "he'll control everything about your future and get you out of my way."

I bet. But I would not willingly tie myself to Guido. "I fail to see how that'll help you, especially going against Dad's decision about the politician. What do you think will happen to you when he finds out?" That hated sly grin spread across his face as I goaded him, making the cleft in his chin more apparent. I didn't like his reaction, not one bit. "He'll discover your hand in it. You can't be that foolish to think Dad won't know you were the one to betray him."

"I've got it covered." He glanced at his atrocious watch again. "This was a courtesy warning to give you time to mentally prepare for your wedding and what'll follow." He winked. "Guido will be here to collect you within the hour."

After dropping that panic-inducing timeline on me, he left. The door clicked loudly as it closed, and the silence that followed his departure felt ominous. I had half an hour at most for the drug to wear off enough to get the hell out of there.

I moved any part of my body that hadn't succumbed to numbness. I balled then relaxed my fists, curling my feet while turning this way and that to take in every inch of the room I was in. A dull pain throbbed at my hip, and I pulled down the waistband of my pants to peer at what was wrong. The sight of a bandage brought back how I'd fallen on the broken shards of the vase when Ricco had manhandled me. Tugging a corner of the tape back, I winced at the poor stich job. *That'll scar horribly.*

There was nothing I could do but keep it covered and clean. I stuck the corner of tape back to my skin and pushed the injury from my mind to take stock of what was really important—how I was going to escape. And to do that, I needed to gather all the information of my surroundings that I could.

The walls were bare but for a small blurry scratch in a one-inch section of drywall where the doorjamb met the wall. Was it a name carved into the drywall or a symbol? It wouldn't have been visible if the door was swung open. I couldn't make out if it was significant.

I knew precisely where Ricco had brought me—away from the house and into a club owned by the family in the heart of Manhattan. Those particular rooms were deep in the bowels of the earth. The steel door led to a windowless room with only a narrow cot and a drain in the middle of the floor—one of the holding cells for when women were brought in before assimilating into the back rooms of the club as sex workers. I was repulsed.

At night, the hallways crawled with men who had access to the rooms—and the drugged women within. Some of the women would remain there until they died. The club was the perfect cover for the depraved customers who ventured down there.

I'd only snuck into that area once before, when my plan to shut down the sex trafficking ring had been in its infancy. I had to take action. I shook away the past, the concern for those locked behind these doors, and the fact that I was no help to them. Not today. And not like this.

Despite the fear of what could happen to me, I kept moving and gaining more control, the anesthetized sensation ebbing as the minutes ticked by. When I could sit up and fully move my arms, I searched for any weapons Ricco could have missed that I'd hidden under my clothes.

The knife sheathed to my arm was gone, and he'd found the ones strapped to my thigh, the gun, and the blade tethered to my forearm beneath the sleeve of my sweater. My breath came faster as panic kicked in, but I held it at bay. There were things he wouldn't know.

I yanked the hem of my sweater up to access the underwire of my black lace bra. The wire was thicker than it should have been, but he wouldn't have noticed that. I concentrated my efforts on two small slits on the inside where the curved metal began. I pried the small tool from within the hollowed-out support using my nails. With one from the right and then the left, I had tools to pick the lock.

I slipped off my shoes then used my nail to depress the hidden button near the base of the stiletto, and the encasement slid off to reveal a sharply pointed dagger in place of the heel. I clutched my meager weapons then pushed myself off the bed on shaky legs and tiptoed to the door, not knowing how much time had passed. My heart pounded, and my limbs shook. Before I attempted the lock, I peered at the mark scratched into the paint on the wall. Bile climbed my throat. *I know what that is and who put it there.*

It was a tiny chamomile flower, representing strength in adversity, the same one my mom used to draw or etch into anything she wanted me to pay close attention to. The same one was on the necklace I wore and the jewelry box where we used to leave each other notes and trinkets that I'd relocated into a getaway bag.

What the hell was she doing in a holding cell?

I rested my head on the door and took several deep breaths. I couldn't afford to get distracted. The mystery of why the flower was there would have to wait another day when I was far away from this place.

Once I regulated my emotions, I carefully threaded the tools into the lock, working them silently, listening and feeling for the click that would free me. When it happened, I jumped to my feet with my stiletto in hand, the dangerous blade facing out. Yanking the door open as hard and fast as I could, I pushed through the threshold as the lone guard stationed in the hall turned, his hand on his gun.

He was taller than Ricco but not wider. My left hand curled around his forearm to slow his momentum. I couldn't match his strength. I had one chance, and I was taking it.

I fell against him. He caught me. Using his confusion, I swung with all my might and sank the razor-sharp blade into his throat then tugged down. A gurgling sound escaped his lips. Using all my weight, I jerked him toward the room's entrance. He crumpled to the floor as he clutched the gushing wound. Eyes wide, he tried to staunch the flow of blood that pulsed from where I'd stuck him in the carotid artery.

I didn't feel bad. He worked for Ricco, and my best interests were not his concern.

As I stepped over him and kicked his weapon away, he weakly made a grab for my shoe. The bulk of his body kept the door firmly open. I wedged my other stiletto in the crack of the doorway, not caring that it cut into the leather. I needed that door to stay where it was.

His legs would be the easiest to move, so I grabbed both behind the knees, stepped fully into the room, and spun his body so there was enough space for the door to close. Like dead weight, his legs hit the ground when I released them. I retrieved the gun and tucked it into the back of my pants. Blood pooled beneath the guard as his life slowly ebbed.

I yanked the blade from his neck and then cleaned it on his clothes before slipping the outer casing back into place. My tools went back into the hollowed-out wires—I couldn't take the chance of losing them in case I had to break out of somewhere else. I peeked around the door and listened. After a few seconds, when I didn't hear any alarms, I carefully closed the door behind me.

If I could reach the exit, I knew I would make it. It wasn't far. But time was working against me. I raced down the empty hallway with my shoes in hand, blocking the ominous doors and the women who might be behind them from my mind. The best way for me to help them was to get out of there.

As I skidded around a corner that led to the stairwell, deep voices filtered down the corridor. I was two floors below the exit to the alleyway. My heart jackhammered against my ribs as I shoved hard off the balls of my feet. When I grasped the push bar to access the stairwell, the distinctive sound of Guido's laugh trilled much too close.

Fear crawled along my spine. I pushed the bar then slipped inside just as I caught movement from the corner of my eye. I eased the door shut with great care, trying not to make a sound, then gripped the railing to support my shaking legs as I fled up the two flights of stairs.

My ears strained for any sound of pursuit. *Could I have gotten lucky enough that they hadn't seen me?* God, I hoped so. But even if I had, they would find the dead guard and the fact that I was missing. I had minutes—possibly seconds—until they sounded the alarm and dragged me back.

The cold metal beneath my hands taunted me with freedom as I pushed with all my might. I burst from the building, and arctic-cold air slapped me in the face. The icy pavement froze my feet. I allowed myself a few blinks to adjust to the brightness of the morning as I took a precious second to slip on my heels. Rough brick scratched my palm as I leaned against it. Once my feet were covered, I raced through the alley. At the end, I joined the crowds of intelligent people bundled in coats, hats, and scarves against the elements on the sidewalk.

My current path would take me to the trains. They wouldn't expect me to do that. In their eyes, hailing a cab or calling for a car and going to my father to inform him of what Ricco had done would make more sense—or so I hoped. Either way, I needed to lose myself in a crowd and become invisible.

Shivers wracked my body, and my breath fogged the air. With each yard I gained, I checked off what I'd done and what had to be accomplished to disappear. The escape path had been set in motion when I'd found the key Mom had hidden for me beneath the jewelry box drawer. Once I'd figured out what it had unlocked and where, I added to the stash of money and weapons she'd left me within the locker. I'd hid the key nearby in case of an emergency that would keep me from going home.

Time passed in agonizing slowness as I sprinted down the steps to the trains, weaving around people. Once on board, I fell into a seat, careful to keep my head down. I needed a disguise— a hat, a coat, something to cover my hair. As the train sped to the next stop, I studied the passengers. It was warmer inside but not enough for people to remove their coats. A newspaper lay on one of the seats, abandoned. I leaned forward and picked it up. It would have to do. There were cameras, and I needed to stay off them so Ricco wouldn't be able to find me.

It was a short trek from the train to the bus terminal where everything was stashed. The key was hidden nearby. It wouldn't be long until I came to the stop where I could retrieve everything Mom and I had hidden in the locker. Thank God I'd overheard Ricco's conversation with Dad.

There was only one place I could go to regroup: the Cayman Islands and to Nico La Rosa, the man who could be my salvation—or my ultimate destruction.

CHAPTER TWO

NICO

Dark clouds gathered miles from the Caribbean Sea's shore, contrasting with the blue skies directly overhead. It would have been wise to stay indoors, but I'd been in meetings most of the morning and had to escape the confinement of four walls and endless bullshit. Besides, the climate fit my mood. I felt a certain symmetry with the volatile storm.

I stood at the railing of my family's waterfront property, tracking the storm's progression and feeling the same uncontrollable electric current building inside me but with no outlet. It'd been like that for a while, and a sense of unfulfillment gnawed at me. Something had to change. I couldn't figure out what.

A warm breeze gusted off the choppy water, bringing a distinct chill on the backend. The temperature was dropping. My guess was about an hour until the skies opened with thunderous wrath over the island.

I still wore dress pants and a white button-down from my last meeting, but I unbuttoned the top few and rolled the sleeves to my elbows to shed the sense of constraint. After taking off my shoes and socks, I followed the steps from our property to the boardwalk that led to the beach. The worn wood beneath my feet acted as an anchor, grounding me in the moment as I took in the island's beauty. Waves crashed against the shore, tearing at the sand and slowly revealing the coastline we would see once everything blew over. In the storm's aftermath, there would exist a reminder of surprises around every corner.

I was concerned that the New York Mafia syndicate would be one such surprise—an unwelcome one. The Amato and Tucci families couldn't pose a problem that we were aware of, but the Verretti family had been working with us as of late, making connections and helping out when we needed answers, particularly about the Amato family. I wasn't entirely comfortable with the toehold Dante Verretti had gained in the Chicago Mafia. It was clear that the Verrettis should be the ones running New York, speaking for the other crime families and serving as a voice in commissions.

If that happened, it would cause an uproar in Italy, where another family or two were losing power and vying to position themselves to join us in Chicago. But I couldn't figure which was the greater of the two evils—which family would benefit ours as an ally and make us even more formidable?

Withdrawing my phone from my pocket, I pressed the contact button for Marco, my eldest sibling and the boss of our family. He picked up on the second ring, and I got right to the point.

"Have you learned any more about the Verretti family?" They were the strongest of the three New York families but nothing compared to the power mine had in Chicago.

"Not much, other than Dante held up his end of the deal and transported Guido back to his father."

Leo Amato, Guido's father, was the boss of the New York Mafia that we considered to be the least of a threat between the three that resided there. Guido, the former underboss, had caused nothing but problems for Luc's wife, Summer. After everything that had gone down several weeks before in December, we all hoped that would be the last we saw of him. Because if he dared to step foot in our territory again, he would leave in a body bag.

"Something isn't adding up. Guido Amato wants to knock off his father and assume his place in the family. That much is clear. But Dante and the Verretti family could be in league with the Tucci boss. Have you been able to confirm there isn't a connection? Because the interactions the Five Families have had with Dante have positioned his family so they could broker an alliance with us."

"Where's this coming from?" Marco's deep voice vied with the thunder that rumbled in the distance, with a few lightning strikes venturing closer. I could picture my brother shoving a hand through his dark hair as he stood to scan the perimeter visible from the window of the mansion where he lived with his wife, El.

"I've done some digging into the Tucci family. There was a contract offered to Dante for an arranged marriage with Mia. Has he said anything about it?"

"No. Our discussions have centered around the Amatos." A clatter sounded as if Marco had tossed a pen onto his desk. "The few times Mia has been brought up, Dante was cagey, and lately, there's been a hint of panic. It was brief, but I caught it. If she fled, and he'd changed his mind and planned to marry her... you could be right. He's hiding something regarding Mia Tucci. We need to proceed with caution and do more digging before we deem them allies."

"I wrapped up business here"—my job had been to check on the bank we owned and see what we had in the vault—"but I'm going to stay a few more days and hack the Tucci and Verretti accounts." In my gut, I felt as if Mia was the key. But before I could determine whether that was correct, I had to dig into all their secrets. A lot could be uncovered by following the money trail.

In the background, I could hear another phone ringing. Marco asked me to hold. As I waited, I let my focus drift back to the brewing tempest, and I soaked up its turbulent, rejuvenating energy. Lightning strobed in jagged lances, striking the ground not far from the house with a deafening boom. Thunder crackled through the air as smoke rose from where the bolt had struck. A large body appeared around the corner of the house as I stood with my back to the water. It was one of the guards, rushing toward me.

A skeleton security crew was with me, staying in the guesthouse. Geo came toward me then stopped, his mouth a grim slash on his scowling face.

"The electrical panel with the security lines took a hit. Mike will work on repairing it, but it may be a day or two."

"We should be fine." Only my family knew I was there. I wasn't worried and turned back to watch the storm's progression as Geo raced back to help Mike. I should have gone in, but I wasn't ready.

"Nico."

I snapped back, keying in on the tension in Marco's voice. "I'm here."

"That was Tony. A bomb went off outside of Envy."

Tony Caruso, Max's brother, managed the nightclubs the Five Families owned. He'd stepped sideways in the family when his older brother returned from the dead, ultimately taking over as boss of the Caruso family.

My fingers tightened on my phone, the threat to my family a dark shadow sweeping through me and demanding the need for retribution. "Was anyone hurt? And do they know who planted it?"

"Max and Lil were caught in the blast. From what Tony said, their injuries are surface. We should have news on who attacked us within the hour. You're staying there for a few more days?"

"Two. But I can come back now."

"No," Marco growled. "Not yet. Do what you can from there."

Follow the chatter and look for money exchanging hands. That was what Marco meant, and I was damn good at it. I would do my part from the Caribbean and find those fuckers who dared to harm any within the family.

"Keep me posted."

"I will." I hung up then slipped my phone back into my pocket. On the horizon, dense, dark clouds moved closer, casting shadows on the beach where I stood. Lightning strobed in the sky, not quite daring to reach for the earth a second time. That explained why I was the only person out there. Rain beat down on the crashing waves in the distance as the wind picked up, howling over the angry landscape.

The change happened in minutes and would have rendered my conversation with my brother impossible to hear. The wind hurdled sea spray as my mind rolled with questions about the connection between Mia and Dante and whether they could be involved in what had happened outside of the club. My gut told me that such a connection existed, and whatever it was, the hidden truth of whether we could trust the Verretti family or if they were plotting our destruction would reveal itself.

I tracked the progression of the approaching storm and the streaks of lightning that pierced the dark clouds. Jagged bolts stabbed the horizon. Electricity charged the air, adding to the sense of impending danger. Sea spray misted over me, and the taste and scent of rain permeated my every breath. I wanted to stay on the shoreline longer, tempting the fates. But the sting of sand from the howling wind forced me to head back and watch the storm from the lanai.

I turned and stopped short, staring at the barrel of a 9mm

pointed at my chest from two feet away. Long black hair tangled in the wind, partially obscuring the woman's face, but if I had any doubt who it was, it left with the flash of violet eyes. Mia Tucci hadn't wanted to be found, but she was standing next to me.

CHAPTER THREE

MIA

The wind howled, and lightning strobed in the distance, followed immediately by the sharp clap of thunder. Silvery light danced over Nico's chiseled features, highlighting an angular jaw that could have cut glass. His pictures hadn't done him justice—even the ones I'd hidden beneath the floorboard that I'd loosened under my bed. I'd even created a full-blown fantasy over the years, with Nico as my knight in shining armor, a man who loved me unconditionally—me, the one nobody thought twice about unless they wanted to use me for their gain. I took another second to study him. The images I coveted, stolen from my father's reports, had failed to accurately account for how his flashing dark eyes, his alluringly crooked grin, or the faint dimple on his left cheek would affect me in person.

I stood opposite him, my legs shoulder-width apart, steadily aiming my gun at him. Exhaustion weighed heavily on me as sand pelted and stung my exposed arms, helping to keep me awake and focused. "Hello, Nico." I studied him from behind my weapon.

His hands were in his pockets, and he appeared relaxed and

unthreatened. Nico was the quiet one in the family. Fiercely loyal but brutal, just like the rest of the members of the Five Families. I had a deal to broker specifically with him—my life depended on it.

"Mia."

"I need a favor." There was no reason to dance around the issue.

Nico's gaze hardened and dropped from mine to the Glock then back again. "And the gun is supposed to make me more amiable to your request?"

"It's just a precaution." I hoped with every fiber of my being that he would honor my gesture of good faith from a month before, when I'd alerted Summer that the Amato family had entered Chicago and was after her. I knew them and what they would have done if they'd gotten their hands on her. It wouldn't have been pretty, and I didn't wish that even on my worst enemies.

One thing I did know, thanks to my habit of sneaking into Dad's office and reading his PI files at three in the morning, was that was that Summer—an employee of Luc's California firm whom he'd brought to Chicago when he joined the family as the new Brambilla boss—had been protected. The Chicago Mafia hadn't been aware of the danger waiting in the wings, and I'd managed to warn her in the tiny window of time available. Could they have saved her? Possibly, but I'd risked so much to make sure she did. "The families owe me."

"You mean Luc owes you."

I narrowed my eyes, trying to keep a clear line of sight amidst my hair, which tangled around my face in the wind. I raised my voice, battling the weather. "I know how things work with the families, so no, I mean you."

Nico smirked, and I knew I would need a show of faith to get him to see me as more than an enemy. *Here goes nothing.* I lowered the gun to my side, unwilling to set it down and hoping that was enough for him. "Can we talk?"

A moment passed before he notched his head toward the boardwalk. I backed up one step then another. When he maneuvered to my left side and took my arm, I let him, too stunned by the jolt of electricity at his touch to attempt to shake him off. It was a concession—at least that was what I told myself.

I gripped my gun in my right hand but kept it trained on the ground. If he tried to take it from me, I would fight him. I refused to think that there was a chance he could overpower me. I had to tell myself that I would shoot him if he tried. I wasn't taking any chances. Too much was at stake, and I had to remain one step ahead of everyone.

Trusting him even that much was a risk, and I hoped he didn't cross me. I would shoot him if I had to. I'd been backed into that proverbial corner for so long that I barely remembered what it was like to feel any way other than desperate.

I'd dressed for the hot weather typical of the island, not expecting the chill from the storm, and goose bumps dotted my exposed arms. Heat radiated from Nico's body, which helped suppress a full-body shiver from overtaking mine.

The sky continued to darken as the thick clouds moved overhead, the crack and boom of thunder almost instantaneously following lightning strobing across the sky. The scent of rain permeated the air. I hurried my steps, and Nico matched my speed. The house wasn't far as the first fat raindrops fell, splashing us and the worn boardwalk. We dashed up the steps at a pace that left me breathless.

I hadn't slept in a long time. Since dawn, I'd hidden just out of reach of camera range on the outskirt of the estate where I'd learned Nico was staying, waiting for my opportunity. It'd come when he'd gone to the beach for a short walk before the storm struck and lightning had damaged one of the electrical boxes, keeping his guards busy. My fingers tingled from the rush of adrenaline suddenly coursing through me as we reached the edge of the patio and an infinity pool that took up a large portion of the outdoor living.

As we skirted around the rippling water of the dark-blue pool, Nico indicated for me to take one of the seats under the overhang just before the sliders that led into the house. *I guess we're staying outside.* I settled onto a cushioned patio chair, my back angled to the rear corner of the space, protected against someone coming up behind me. I hadn't noticed anyone else in residence other than security walking the perimeter, but it was better to be safe.

There was enough coverage from the wind that I could shove my tangled hair from my face for an unobstructed view of the man who unknowingly held my future in his hands.

When he settled into the chair opposite me, I released my firm grip on the gun but kept it on the chair cushion next to me. I took my hand off it and then flattened my palms on my thighs. It would have been better to approach him without putting him on the defensive, but pulling a gun was the only way I felt safe enough even to get to that point.

I didn't know Nico, not really. But I did know of his reputation. And I was well aware of how a beautiful exterior could hide all degrees of inner ugliness. I did not doubt that he, too, was a monster. All I hoped was that I could reach the protective side that I'd heard all the brothers in the La Rosa family had for their sister and extended to the women of the Mafia family.

"We're here. You've got my attention." His whiskey-colored eyes narrowed, and power crackled in the air from his predatory presence, making the fine hairs on the back of my neck rise. "What do you want, Mia?"

"Protection. Marriage." The words spilled from my lips before I could censor myself and ease into what I needed from him.

His bark of laughter set my nerves further on edge.

I blamed my lack of finesse on exhaustion and the ticking clock I felt deep in my bones. It wouldn't be long before Ricco or Guido found me and dragged me back to hell.

"Why the hell would I do that?" He reined in the harshness of his reaction by pressing his lips together, his eyes flashing with something I couldn't decipher. A moment passed with neither of us saying anything. "We can work something else out without marriage."

I shook my head, fighting the panic rising from his rejection. I had to tell him everything. It was the only way I could get him to agree to my plan. "I'm not safe."

He rose one brow almost mockingly, and I wanted to leap from my chair and land a right hook across that angular jaw. This was not the man I'd fantasized about, the one whose picture I had secreted away in my room.

"None of us are safe. It's the way of our world." He tilted his head to one side, and I felt his penetrating scrutiny—it was as if he could see inside me, and I wasn't sure I liked it. "Each day in this life is a gift. You know that. I can't imagine that the Mafia in New York is much different."

I shook my head, conflicted by his words. "No. I mean yes. It's impossible not to understand that, growing up in our world. But what I'm talking about is much worse."

My fingers dug into the sides of the chair as I told him about Ricco and how he vied for control of our family, how he saw me as an obstacle. I knew I was my father's pawn—he would use me to gain power, marrying me off to who he deemed would benefit him the most, despite how I felt about it or what that meant for my safety. Finally, I painted the picture of my last hours and what I'd overheard my father and Ricco talking about, omitting the part about being drugged and locked up, the flower etching in the room, or what my mom had left me in a train station locker. "I need protection from my family and from the Amatos. No one but you can give that to me."

Silence stretched between us until he broke it with a low growl. I hurried to finish what I had to say, needing him to understand the gravity of my situation and what would fix it. "I won't be safe until I'm fully under the protection of the Five Families. And you damn well know that nothing aside from marrying one of you will give me that."

"Marry Tony. He's single."

I snorted. "I've done my research. He's not as connected."

"He is. Tony is Max's brother."

Max was the boss of the Caruso family. "But not an underboss like you, so no. He wouldn't have enough power to stop them from coming for me." I held his gaze, my soul bared. "It has to be you."

CHAPTER FOUR

NICO

Thunder boomed after Mia's mic-drop statement, and the sky opened fully, dumping sheets of rain that obscured our view beyond the patio's overhanging shelter. I sat across from her, digesting everything she'd told me, weighing the possibility of her involvement in the bomb in Chicago and the logic of her proposal against my anger at the way her family had treated her.

It wasn't uncommon for a Mafia boss to use his daughter as a pawn for power. Hell, it'd happened often enough within the Five Families. If we were to marry, she was correct that she would be protected. But why would I take that plunge? No woman before her had tempted me to do so. I didn't think I had the right makeup to have feelings that lasted after the first time I slept with a woman, despite how much I wished that were different.

I wasn't a boss, but my family was powerful, as was my position. I studied her body language, the tension in her shoulders, and how her fingers were white at the tips from their tight grip on the chair. Dark half-moons hung beneath her otherworldly eyes. I couldn't deny that she'd intrigued me since I learned she'd tipped Summer off to danger.

"This favor. It wipes the slate clean from you warning Summer."

Her heavily lidded eyes widened. "Yes. Do we have a deal?"

I hesitated. "Divorce isn't an option."

"I'm aware."

"The only way to leave is through death."

"Marriage, Mafia… both have the same terms." Her features remained devoid of emotion, steady and penetrating.

I scanned the length of her body, from her midnight hair to the chipped copper polish on her bare toes. A fine sheen of mist from the rain pounding the patio coated us where we faced away from the house. She had to have been cold, but sheer determination held her immobile.

"What will I get out of this?" *Why am I even entertaining this conversation?* "Tying myself to the Tucci family isn't ideal. There needs to be more."

She sank her teeth into her full bottom lip before releasing it, worry swimming in her expressive eyes. "I'll help you take my family down."

I raised my brows. "You have no loyalty to your father?" I wasn't even a little surprised. It wasn't unheard of, but I had to check her motives. Plenty of my closest friends had simply endured under their fathers' rules until the time was right to end it.

"My loyalty to him died when my mother went into the ground." Her voice vibrated with emotion. "All I am to him is a bargaining chip for power. And Ricco"—disgust curled her lip—"he isn't even my blood."

"I won't ally with the Tucci family." Marrying Mia would connect my family to one of our enemies. But there was that saying, the devil on my shoulder argued, to keep your enemies close. And Mia Tucci would be no hardship to have by my side.

I could simply shield her without marriage, which was what I preferred. It was the smarter bet, as I had no intention of taking that plunge unless it was for love or, on the other hand, a substantial gain. But I doubted I would ever find the same love that my parents and siblings had. That wasn't in the cards for me. It never had been.

I wanted to push her and see what else she would reveal. "We don't need your help to take down the Tucci family. Nor is it a priority."

"I get it. You don't think they're a threat. But combined with the Amatos, which is what I'm sure my not-brother has planned, they could be."

"Doubtful." The only New York family that concerned me was the Verrettis—Dante in particular. And the rest of the Five Families, including Marco, were considering an alliance. I wasn't convinced that was a smart move, though, until we did more digging.

"Are you aware of the sex workers my father has in his club? Of the women he traffics?" Palm tree fonds whipped against moody gray skies. In the distance, waves crashed angrily.

A jolt of fury tore through my body, and I fought the urge to jump to my feet. *Emiliana.* I'd once had a crush on the Mafia princess, Enzo Vitale's sister, but my feelings had been no match for Stefano's. She was never mine.

She'd endured—overcome—a lot. We had some intel on the Tucci family sex ring, but the mere mention shook my resolve. I hadn't been on the team who'd rescued Emiliana and slayed those who had wronged her and all the others. No one in the families forgave themselves for what had happened to her. It never should have occurred. The rat who'd betrayed her had paid. But it wasn't enough.

"What about it?" The words were deep and garbled—anger lashed them from my throat without restraint.

"I'm the key to take it down for good. To make my family pay for what they're doing."

I studied Mia—the way she leaned forward, the disgust that curled her lip, and the darkness that filtered through her eyes, turning them almost purplish-blue. Some emotion that I couldn't quite grasp swam in the tanzanite depth. *The desire for revenge?*

The bargaining chip she'd presented to convince me to give her the protection she needed was enough for me to sacrifice my freedom, to put an end to something our families abhorred. "How are you the key?" I fought myself from saying yes, needing to interrogate her further. She wasn't an ally—not yet, anyway. I could not trust her.

"I know how to get in undetected. Where they keep the women and when they ship them out."

"Why not work with Dante?" The Verretti boss would have been the most logical option for her. He was powerful enough to give her the protection she needed... and he was in the same state.

"He knows some of what I do, but he didn't offer me the safety that you could. My father already approached him with an arranged marriage. He turned it down." Hurt swam in her eyes. "I can't go to him. The only way to keep my family at bay is if you marry me. Then I promise"—her words hissed through clenched teeth—"we'll take them down together."

"Tell me now, and I'll make that happen without marriage." The rain had increased its fury, and my clothes clung to my body, despite the protective overhang. We needed to go inside soon. But before I took Mia, an enemy and virtual stranger, into my domain, this thing needed to be settled.

"No." Her body tensed, and she straightened as if she would bolt. But there was nowhere to go, not in that weather. "My deal is marriage. Your full protection. I won't disclose anything until after the vows are said and the ink is dry."

I shook my head, a short huff leaving my parted lips. That wasn't the only way to get the information.

She narrowed her eyes. "I know what you're thinking, and I can withstand torture. You won't get anything out of me until I'm ready to give it. And that'll be when we're officially married—and *all* the families are informed."

Is it worth my freedom? Visually, I swept her again, noting the electricity—not from the storm but that sizzled between us. There was an undeniable attraction there. But none of that mattered if she double-crossed me. And if it came down to that, I would make her life hell before I ended it.

If I was going to sacrifice myself to both a loveless marriage and an enemy, I had some demands. "This marriage will not be in name only."

She gasped then immediately schooled her features until they were devoid of emotion. "Of course. But"—she fidgeted—"can we wait to consummate it until we've gotten to know each other better?"

I nodded. It wasn't an unreasonable request. "We have a temporary deal." I felt the weight of my words settle heavily around my shoulders. I was doing it for Emiliana. It was a small way to help, even though nothing would erase what had happened to her. And even though she wasn't mine, she was a good friend.

"When?"

I grinned, amused by her assertiveness. "In two days. We'll fly to Chicago. If you want the families to know, it'll have to be there, with all the bosses present—if I fully agree to this."

The color, what there was, leached from her face. "All? I hardly think it's wise to invite my father. And I'll need an agreement to help you with my family."

"The bosses of the Five Families. The wedding will be in secret, aside from them. We'll need witnesses." I paused, wanting to catch any flicker in her reaction to what I was about to say. "Our marriage will be an act of war against your family. I'll make it clear to your father that I'm taking you without the benefit of my family's power added to his."

Melodic laughter dripping in malice spilled from her lips. "I want to be there when you tell him that."

I inclined my head. I had no problem with that. But there were things I did. I unfurled from the chair and prowled toward her. I stood before her then leaned down, bracing on the arms of her chair, moving toward her until our eyes were inches apart. "If you attempt to betray me at any point, I'll withdraw my protection and turn the Five Families against you. You'll wish for death long before you draw your last breath."

A shiver coursed through her body, but she held my gaze without wavering. "I understand."

I understand. Not "I'll never betray you." Clever. I wouldn't underestimate her.

"Trust has to be earned." When my fingers closed around the gun that rested beside her, removing it from her reach, she didn't flinch. Her chin notched higher. I set it on the table then helped her to her feet. I ran my hands over every inch of her body in a slow, thorough manner, stripping away an arsenal of weapons, placing each on the table before I guided her to the sliding door. We needed to get into dry clothes.

Once inside, I led her to the bathroom and handed her a towel.

"What will you tell my father about us, when you agree?" She waited for my response, her piercing eyes narrowed, with the towel as a barrier in front of her.

"Nothing. I don't answer to him. He'll learn we're married after the fact. If he has questions, they'll go unanswered." I left her standing there. My sister, Sofia, kept clothes at the house, and I was sure Mia would appreciate something warm and dry. I grabbed the first thing I saw from the closet and brought it back to her. "After you shower, come find me in the kitchen."

I didn't wait for a response, but I caught the quiet click of the door as it shut and the lock engaged. I grinned, amused by the turn of events. Mia was a beautiful woman, but I wouldn't touch her until after we were married. And only then if she agreed. I'd meant what I said about our marriage not being in name only. Even so, I would never force myself on a woman.

Once in my room, I stripped out of my clothes then put on dry pants and a shirt. I had a few things to do before we left the island and hoped for some insight into whether she would make an attempt on my life.

I exited my room. As I passed the bathroom, the faint sound of the shower breeched the closed door. She'd looked like she was about ready to pass out if not for sheer determination. Another wave of fury burned through me as I considered the situation she'd fled. But most of all, I needed to find out who had told her where I was.

CHAPTER FIVE

NICO

Ice clinked against the sides of my glass as I poured whiskey just shy of the rim. I took a sip, relishing the burn as it slid down my throat. I'd let an enemy into my home and would soon give her access to my family—all in the name of revenge to clear my conscience for not doing more for a friend. That wasn't the only reason, though. Having Mia close would allow me to find out who'd attacked the family with a bomb at the club.

It was risky, but I didn't see that it would cost me much to protect her, to have her by my side.

I wasn't convinced she was innocent. Her connection to Dante could have been an elaborate scheme his family and the Tuccis had concocted, so for the time being, I would keep her close. The wedding would occur once Marco approved of it, and if it became necessary, she would leave the union through death.

There was a slight scuff against the marble floor, and I turned to see Mia enter the open-concept space in a pair of formfitting black pants and a flowy sleeveless shirt. Slicked back from her face, her long black hair hung past her shoulders, making her exotic features even more prominent. She appeared young, and if I hadn't looked too closely at the secrets swirling within her eyes, I would have thought she was innocent.

But no one born into our world was free.

"How old are you?" I should have known. And I probably had at one point, but we didn't pay close attention to the New York Mafia.

"Twenty." She notched her chin higher. "Which in our world is old as sin."

I lifted my glass in a toast to the truth of her statement. "Do you want anything to drink? Or eat?"

"Water would be great." She climbed onto a chair that bellied up to the large island.

After setting a glass of water in front of her, I leaned back against the counter with the island between us. Without any makeup, the half-moons beneath her eyes were even darker. *When had she last slept?*

Her gaze darted from the windows to the sliding glass door then returned to me.

Does she think her stepbrother or Guido will come for her on the island? "They won't find you here."

"I was looking at the weather." She stifled a yawn.

I didn't believe her for one second. Hands flat on the cool marble, I leaned forward. "For this to work, there can't be any secrets between us." I waited for her to acknowledge me. "How did you learn where I was?"

"A girl has to have some secrets." The glass knocked against the counter as she set it down unsteadily. Her eyes went half-mast.

I snorted at her answer. Honestly, it was something my sister would have said. I decided to let Mia keep her little secret for the time being. I would find out soon enough if she wanted me to go through with her crazy scheme. "We're leaving tomorrow night. Why don't you get some sleep?"

She slid off the chair without a word and went to the guest

room I'd shown her earlier. And with Mia asleep—because by the way she looked, she would be as soon as her head hit the pillow—I could do some digging into what else she was hiding.

***

Mia

I was exhausted as I locked and barricaded the door with a chair under the knob then climbed into the guest room bed and snuggled under the covers, fully clothed. Even though Nico could have killed me already if he'd wanted to, I had a hard time trusting anyone.

I'd studied more than just his photo before coming here. He liked numbers and algorithms, sometimes more than people. That didn't make him oblivious to body language or interactions, at least not from what I could tell. Often, the quiet ones were deadliest. I was counting on that for my benefit.

Too tired to think about our tentative arrangement, I closed my eyes, falling asleep almost instantly. But it didn't take long until anxiety built, manifested in my dreams, and caused me to toss and turn. The sheets tangled around my legs like vines, securing me in place and making me vulnerable to the monster outside my door.

Caught in a deep sleep in the midst of a dream that catapulted me to a dark memory, I tensed as a board, the one Ricco forgot about more often than not, squeaked. I couldn't move. Like many times before, it felt as if a weight immobilized me.

A click sounded. The lock was released. Then a faint light pierced the inky darkness. My stepbrother had breached the one place where I should have been safe. I was desperate to spring from the bed and to safety, but I wouldn't make it in time. I slid my hand under the pillow, curling my fingers around the knife I kept there. My breath escaped in small pants as my body tensed.

His steps were light. I eased the knife to the side of the pillow. My eyelids mere slits, I tried to maintain the illusion of sleep. The pounding of my heart was so loud that I feared he could hear it too.

I felt malevolence radiating from his body as he slithered through the darkness. He was close. I held my breath until I felt the brush of his hand on my arm, then sprang into action, arcing the knife and sinking it deep into him. The pressure on my prone arm left. His hand sliced up. Sharp pain exploded against my wrist. His blade never connected.

"You little bitch," Ricco growled too close to my face, his hand gripping my wrist so hard that I dropped my only weapon.

I opened my mouth to scream as his other hand slapped over it in a punishing seal. Pain shot through my thighs as he held me in place by kneeling on me with one leg. He yanked my wrists together with a zip tie. Duct tape replaced his hand over my mouth. He hauled me out of bed. My back to his chest, I kicked wildly, connecting with his shin in a satisfying thud.

The more I struggled, the tighter his arm around my ribs became, restricting my diaphragm and lungs. He held a rag over my nose, and I tried to jerk back from the sweet-smelling liquid —*chloroform*. Spots peppered my vision, blocking the small light from somewhere in the hallway as I became increasingly disoriented. We were moving, my legs dangling uselessly several feet from the ground.

I tried, but the darkness spread the more I inhaled, my entire body tingling until I slipped into unconsciousness.

When I came to, it was to smooth leather beneath my cheek, a drug-induced headache, and the subtle movement of a car speeding down a road. A wave of dizziness swept over me, and I inhaled with measured breaths to dispel the effects of the chloroform.

There were no overhead streetlights. We had to have been on a highway. I took stock of who else was in the car. The passenger seat was empty. He'd thrown me in the back. The only good thing about it was the absence of the tape over my mouth, no doubt so that it wouldn't leave a mark that he couldn't lie his way out of if my father asked.

I shifted with careful movements, bringing my legs down to the floor mat and positioning myself behind him. That was when I noticed the black silk dress with sequins that I had on. Horror shot through me—he'd changed my clothes. Saliva pooled in my mouth, and I repeatedly swallowed, unwilling to throw up and alert him that I was awake.

A renewed sense of survival filled me, and I blocked everything from my mind, inching close to his seat. Before he could stop me, I lurched and slipped my bound hands over his head. As soon as I had them lowered and positioned at his neck, I raised my knees and leaned back, leveraging my weight for maximum effect on his throat, choking him.

The car swerved. His hand grabbed mine and squeezed so hard that I thought the bones would snap, but I didn't release the pressure. Brakes squealed, and the car jerked to the right then to a stop on the shoulder of the road. His hands dug into my wrists, wrenching me off before he pulled me forward and threw me over the seats. My back hit the dash with a painful thud. He threw the car in park as I scrambled for purchase, attempting to flip over and get my feet under me.

Ricco's cruel gaze met mine before he pinned me down against the car seat, reaching for something on the passenger's floor. I caught the glint of glass before he fisted the hair at my nape and forcefully tilted my head back. He pried open my mouth while I struggled. Vodka flooded my throat. I tried to spit it out, but he fought me as I gagged. I choked on the fiery trial of alcohol until it no longer burned.

The more that went down my throat, the weaker my

struggle became. Danger flashed in my mind, and my pulse thrummed a subdued beat as he set the bottle down. My entire body shook. With the last of my strength, I struggled against him.

I balled my fist when he cut the zip tie and thrust upward. When it met solid contact, I didn't stop—my only goal was to break free. Something buzzed in my ear. slicing through the blind haze of terror. The sound became progressively louder until I could make out the shouting.

"Mia!"

My open palm cracked against a face hovering inches from mine. Part of me registered it wasn't Ricco, but the dream—*the memory*—had its claws in deep. Nico held my wrists loosely but tightly enough to stop me from hitting him.

With no hand over my mouth, I let loose the scream that had built from the moment Ricco breached the dream realm.

I knew it was a nightmare, but I couldn't shake the sense of life-threatening danger of what I'd gone through at fifteen years old. Using Nico's grip as leverage, I pushed sideways against his hold, trying to widen our arms and decrease the space between us. Then I whipped my head forward. My forehead collided with his in a dull thud as stars exploded behind my eyes.

I twisted, not letting it kill my advantage, attempting to break free. Strong arms wrapped around me, lifting me from the bed. Jolts of electricity traveled up my arms from the contact of his hands as he attempted to still me.

"Mia, goddammit! Stop."

My surroundings trickled in, grounding me. There was no car, no road where my hated stepbrother had tossed me. My blood was free of alcohol.

The hammering of my pulse against my throat eased. Soft light spilled through the sliding glass doors as the sun crested the horizon. It was morning, not the dead of night. and I took comfort in the fact that the man who held me was Nico, not my despised and abusive not-brother.

Where Nico's hands touched me, my body sizzled. I lurched back, unsettled. "I'm fine. Let go." My words were hoarse, pushed past clenched teeth and a raw throat. As soon as his hands loosened, I jerked away from him. I put a few feet between us, shifting so the open sliders through which he'd entered the room were to my back. His dark eyes swirled, and I shivered from the intensity.

He wore a pair of gray sweats and no shirt. I didn't need to look to know he had a gun in the back waistband. Christ. He was chiseled, solid—so much muscle. I kept my gaze locked onto his, unwilling to let him see I was even a little affected by his touch. Nothing good would come of revealing the slightest weakness.

"What the fuck was that?"

The fine hairs on my body rose, registering the threat in his tone, but I didn't know him well enough to tell whether the threat was directed at me. "Nothing. A bad dream. Night terrors." I waved the incident away, attempting to downplay the hell I'd been trapped in. "It's best to leave me alone if they come. It'll pass."

"Bullshit." He held still, his body tense.

I shrugged, trying to appear calm. "I don't know what you want to hear. I remember nothing. Never do. That's how night terrors work."

His gaze narrowed before he stood, towering over me. I should have felt intimidated by the fury that rolled off him in waves. Oddly, I didn't. But I should have. The guy I'd obsessed over in reports and pictures while trapped in my father's house more often than not wasn't the same version as the flesh and blood one. When he scrubbed a hand down his face then through his hair, I trailed his movements. There was enough space between us, and I wanted to keep it that way.

"You're lying. And sooner or later, you will tell me what happened that caused you to wake up fighting like that." His hand dropped to his side, and several seconds ticked by before he pivoted to the open door. "I'm making coffee and food. Come eat. Or don't."

I didn't move. I barely breathed. My entire body felt like it'd been in the presence of a predator. That Nico was a member of one of the deadliest Mafia families in Chicago proved how just my reaction was. But the sense of danger was different. I never wanted to cross him.

Before he ruthlessly yanked the chair loose to open the door and pass into the hallway, he caught my gaze over his shoulder. I froze, locked in the fierceness of brown eyes swirling with black. "If you want my protection, you'll come clean. I don't need to get tangled up with your family. I won't risk more than I already have."

CHAPTER SIX

NICO

Anger made my movements stiff as I got the coffee going. I didn't need the caffeine based on the jolt of adrenaline from the first ear-shattering scream Mia had let loose minutes before the sun rose. What the hell had happened to her? Caught in a nightmare, she'd fought me as if her life depended on it.

My gut warned that more was happening behind the scenes with Mia, which meant it was time to reach out to my brother before she joined me in the kitchen. I couldn't promise her that we would marry for her protection unless I cleared it with the boss of our family, mainly due to who her father was.

With a cup of strong coffee, I let myself out onto the patio, where I would have privacy.

I tapped Marco's contact, and he picked up on the third ring.

"Should I be concerned that you're calling me this early?"

Most definitely, but I didn't admit to that. "Any news on who planted the bomb at the club?"

"Yeah, and it's not good." Marco's voice growled through the receiver. "The bomb's signature points to the Verretti family."

A surge of fury rushed through me. *And why is Dante so concerned about finding Mia?* My level of distrust went up a few more notches, as I tallied additional reasons not to trust her. "What's the plan for retaliation?"

"Nothing. Not yet." A door slammed in the distance, and I could make out his wife, Elena's, laugh. "I have a meeting with Dante later today. Something isn't adding up."

"I have news as well. I found Mia Tucci—or rather, she found me."

"Where is she?"

"Here." I glanced inside to make sure she hadn't entered the kitchen yet. "We had a storm, and our security took a lightning strike. It's glitchy at best, which enabled her to come up behind me while I was on the beach."

"That explains why she got the drop on you. But why is she in Grand Cayman?"

"To find me. She wants protection from both the Amatos and her family."

"Joey Tucci will have a problem with that. There has to be a good reason for us to get involved in the mess that'll cause."

I ran my hand through my hair. *This is so messed up.* "She's negotiating a marriage with me for protection in exchange for taking down the Tucci prostitution ring."

Silence met my words as the rippling waves broke gently along the shore. It was pleasant out, but the humidity and temperature would soon rise with the sun.

"It's not a bad idea. If we can take down the ring, we'll weaken the Tucci family with a direct hit to their finances."

I snorted. "They aren't hurting. I spent a little time digging last night. Even if we dismantle the ring, they have other sources that fatten their accounts. Aside from that. I'm all for taking them down, which is why I'm considering marrying Mia."

"It concerns me that she found you there. It's not a well-known destination for us by anyone outside our family." The distinct sound of the coffee machine told me Marco was in the kitchen.

"I'll find out how she accomplished that."

"You're seriously considering this alliance?" Marco drew out his question. "The only way out of marriage is death."

"Hers. Yes. I've thought about that. It's worth the sacrifice to dismantle the trafficking ring."

"Fine. I'll leave the final decision to you. If she's with us, she can divulge a lot about the three New York families. But on the other hand, she could be working with one or more of them to try to take our family down from the inside."

"That crossed my mind too. I'll keep you posted." I disconnected the call then let myself back into the house. I heard the bathroom door open in the guest room. She would be out momentarily.

I looked out the sliders to see Geo hovering and motioned him inside. With a gun strapped to his hip, two in a shoulder holster, and a black baseball cap, he appeared just as threatening as he was.

The sliders opened enough for his large frame to pass through. He stopped about a foot from where I was, near the island. "Hey, boss."

"Any problems?"

He frowned. "We increased the perimeter rotation, but security is still glitchy at best. It should be repaired in a few hours."

I nodded, not too worried. Until Mia, there hadn't been an issue here for as long as I'd been coming with my family. "Thanks for the update."

He left as quietly as he'd come. I grabbed a bowl of precut fruit from the fridge and set it out, aware that Mia most likely heard our conversation. I was leaning against the counter when she emerged from the hallway, wearing white capris and a black scoop-neck shirt with the same gold necklace I'd noticed last night.

Downing my last sip of coffee, I said nothing as she took a seat across from me at the island. I was furious. She was right that we owed her—not marriage, necessarily, but a favor for tipping Summer off to the danger she was in. And though Mia had used it as a negotiation tactic, it hadn't held the weight that the other bomb she'd dropped on me had.

She curled her hands around the mug of coffee I'd placed in front of her. Neither of us said a word as she took her first sip. When she set the cup down, my patience had worn thin.

"There are too many unknowns between us for me even to consider a marriage with you." I bent so that my forearms rested on the island then leaned toward her. "You have one hour to come clean with what that nightmare was about, why you screamed Ricco's name, and the real reason behind running from your family."

From over the rim of her mug, she watched me. After drinking half of the coffee, she set it down, crossed her arms, then leaned on the island, mimicking my pose. She briefly pressed her lips together before huffing out a breath. "That's fair, so long as I have your word that this marriage will go through. That you will protect me."

"Tell me everything. Then I'll give you my answer."

She squinted, clearly not trusting me. "In a blood oath."

I couldn't have stopped the grin if I'd tried. *Well played*. "The oath will include your agreement to tell me everything, not to keep any pertinent information regarding the New York Mafia families from me, and not to divulge any secrets you may learn from the Five Families."

Her nod wasn't enough of a response, but I would get her promise on both points if I put my future on the line by tying it to hers. "Tell me."

"The nightmare is irrelevant."

I took in the stubborn tilt of her chin, wondering if it was worth pushing the point. "Then clue me in to what is important."

"Taking down the trafficking ring."

"I'm well aware of that." I worked to keep my tone level and calm, in complete opposition to the frustration I was feeling. "You have to give me more. Otherwise, I'm washing my hands of this situation right here and now."

Her hand came down with a loud crack on the marble countertop. "I'm giving you a freaking map to take down my family's sex trafficking ring!"

"And you could be a plant that the New York Mafia is using to take down the Five Families! Why did you scream Ricco's name?"

"It was a nightmare," she gritted out from between clenched teeth.

"What did Ricco do?" I used to do the same to Sofia when I wanted answers to something. I'd stay calm but relentlessly ask annoying questions, regardless of her response. Eventually, she would scream the information I wanted. While Sofia could endure torture without giving up even a hint of what was sought, that approach often broke through her barriers. I wasn't threatening, intimidating, or trying to harm her. The relentless line of questioning usually worked.

"He's my stepbrother. What didn't he do during the years we were in the same household?" She shifted her balled fists so they were in her lap and out of my line of sight.

"Why did you scream his name."

"It was a nightmare. Not real. And I don't remember what it was about." She flipped her long black hair over her shoulder. "Why do you care?"

"Because I won't marry you until I know more. Is he your lover?"

She curled her upper lip, looking repulsed.

"What did Ricco do to you?"

"He locked me in a cell!" Her head whipped up, and her eyes, blazing with fury, locked onto mine.

I jerked back. A haze of red settled over my vision, and I had to take several breaths through my nose, trying to calm the hell down before I spoke. "What happened?"

With a shove to spin the barstool, she jumped down then stood so her back was to me while she looked out over the Caribbean Sea.

I didn't like it. Without seeing her expression, I couldn't read her beyond listening for her inflection. Not willing to risk it, I joined her by the sliding glass door. After I unlocked it, I pushed the slider open. Resting my hand lightly on the small of her back, I guided her onto the patio and to the area where we were yesterday.

Once she was seated, her hands digging into the seat's cushion, I took the chair opposite her. A small table separated us, as did the wall that hid her emotions. But a hairline fracture had split the nearly impenetrable surface with her revelation of what Ricco had done. It was a small nick in her armor but enough for me to work with.

"If you want me to help you, I need to know everything. Or else you're giving people like Ricco an advantage, and I doubt that was your goal in approaching me with the marriage proposal."

Her eyes closed, and she seemed to come to a resolution as the tension slowly ebbed from her stiff posture, lowering her shoulders by an inch. "My father planned to marry me to a politician. I don't even know what his name is."

It wasn't a horrible idea, nor was it uncommon, but I wasn't going to say that.

She frowned, her gaze crawling over my face. "I know what you're thinking, but you're wrong. Even if he thought he'd gain more power, which I get, my life would be hanging in the balance. A politician couldn't protect me. Not from the Mafia, and you damn well know that."

True. I nodded because it sounded like her father wouldn't have taken precautions with security, based on her fear of the arrangement. Even so, marrying an outsider wouldn't shield her in case of an ambush. She would have to fight, which I had no doubt she had the skills to do, but her husband would probably be worthless. Worse, he would jeopardize her life.

"That's why you've been MIA, because of an arranged marriage?" I studied the stubborn tilt of her chin before catching a flash of what looked like pain flitter across her features.

"It didn't help. I overheard my father discussing it with Ricco. Something was brewing with Ricco, and it wasn't long until I found out what."

"Don't tell me he wanted to marry you?"

She snorted. "He threw his hat in the pot, but my father wasn't having it. So Ricco did the next best thing—in his eyes, anyway. He brokered a deal with Guido."

"Guido lost his status as the Amato underboss. What would Ricco gain from you marrying him?" It was a long shot unless Guido still planned to off his father then take over the family as boss.

"Right. But he and Ricco were working on a way to regain his position as underboss, and I think they might have been plotting against my dad in a long game."

I leaned back in my chair, studying her. "Your marriage to Guido would tether the Tucci family, with or without Joey as boss."

"It would grant Ricco more time, and I would be out of the way. He's power hungry, cunning, and ruthless. Always has been. Underestimating him never ends well."

"I understand what's going on with the power struggle. Now, tell me about the nightmare." The reason why she'd left was apparent, but there was more to it, evident in her rigid posture and the darkening of her eyes. "I won't bind my family to you when you could be a risk. I want to know it all." I frowned when her eyes went dull, not liking whatever caused the dimming of her fire and strength.

"Ricco ambushed me the morning I decided it was time to try to leave. Nothing good would happen, and I knew, aside from the Verretti family, I had no one in my corner. Even Dante wouldn't be able to help me, not when he'd rejected my father's proposition for an arranged marriage with me."

"How far did you get before Ricco found you?" I didn't like the picture she painted, and anger threatened to demolish my calm outer appearance.

"He got to me before I could leave the house and drugged me. I woke up in a windowless room that contained a cot and nothing else. Ricco came to gloat and tell me Guido was on his way. The drugs had begun to wear off, and as soon as I could, I picked the lock, killed the guard, and fled."

"Was this before or after you warned Summer that Guido had found her?"

"After. I overheard Ricco and Guido talking one day. Ricco had helped Guido find where she'd gone. I thought I should even the playing field, sneak out from under my family's watchful eye with the excuse of spending a few days at a spa and instead fly to Chicago. I'd found and hired someone who looked enough like me from a distance to confuse the guards."

My respect for her went up a notch. While that would have infuriated me if she were mine, I admired her resourcefulness. "Why didn't you approach me or anyone else in my family to negotiate protection when you were in Chicago?"

"I thought I had more time then. It wasn't until a few days ago that I realized I had to get away quickly."

I shouldn't have believed a word out of her mouth—she was the enemy, after all—but for some reason, I did. That didn't make me lower my guard. She could have been lying, working with her family to weaken or sabotage mine. "How did you find me? This house isn't listed in our name." It was a haven away from the Mafia world, something my dad wanted for my mom. We visited at least once a year, and it provided a glimpse into another world. I wouldn't trade mine, but it was different, and Mom seemed to recharge there.

"I told you. I hacked into one of your accounts. It took a while, but"—she shrugged and flashed a slight smirk—"I found you."

So she had. "Who else knows about this house or my being here?"

Her eyes widened, and her hands flattened on her thighs. "No one."

That better have been the case. I narrowed my gaze on her, assessing. It would have been foolish to trust her. "You haven't given me anything concrete about the inner workings of your family's business to stage an effective attack... or to convince me that marriage would be worthwhile."

"That room Ricco had locked me in was one of the holding cells for the women who are brought in before they're trafficked. So you see, I'm your best-case scenario for taking down my family because I've been there."

CHAPTER SEVEN

MIA

I had to reel in my emotions. Nico sat across from me on one of the cushioned patio chairs, a small mosaic table between us and the gorgeous Caribbean Sea as a backdrop. He didn't believe me. I couldn't blame him, but it infuriated me just the same. I hated Ricco, and my dad didn't love me. He used me. I was a pawn to them, nothing more.

There was no one in whom I could confide, not even Dante or his brothers, Cal and Adriano. There hadn't been time to go to them, nor was I sure they would offer me sanctuary. Before the conversation I'd overheard in Dad's office, I would have thought so, but that was before Dante rejected my father's proposition to unite our families through marriage.

I clasped my hands tightly in my lap, willing myself to stay calm. No matter how much I wanted to, I couldn't lash out against Nico's veiled distrust. When his gaze traveled over me from head to foot, I had to work hard to suppress a shiver. He was too intense, a silent predator waiting to strike, and for me, the best line of defense. "Do we have a deal?"

Rather than say anything, he withdrew a pocketknife from his pocket. Flipping it open, he grabbed my hand then turned it palm up. He paused with the blade lightly resting against my skin. "This goes both ways."

I nodded to the dual accountability. The moment felt heavy. I would abide by my word, even if he questioned my intentions. "Yes."

The incision was swift and shallow with a sharp sting of pain. Blood welled along my palm as he made the same cut across his then pressed our hands together. Our blood mixed, our eyes locked, and the weight of the moment hung in the air.

I knew he would want my promise first, so I began. "I swear fealty to you. My loyalty equals yours. And in exchange for your protection, for your legal name, I will take all of your and your family's secrets to my grave. Together, we'll dismantle the Tucci sex ring." I said what he wanted to hear, what I was willing to offer, making a binding promise in exchange for safety.

"From this moment, in tandem with your steadfast loyalty, you're mine to protect in body, mind, and soul."

I read between the lines—should I betray him, he would end my life, severing the bonds of marriage and his ties to me. Despite the ominous threat hanging over my head, the oppressive weight I'd been carrying dissipated. For the first time in years, I enjoyed a modicum of safety. The tension between my shoulders eased, and I flashed Nico a smile as he released my hand.

He went into the kitchen only to return with a cloth that he pressed to the small wound on my palm. "We leave for Chicago late this afternoon. The wedding will be tomorrow morning."

I sat up straighter. "Good. Thank you, Nico." I rubbed my fingers over my right temple, feigning discomfort. "Hey, I'm going to lie down for a while. I've got a headache."

He didn't respond, but I felt his eyes on me the entire way until I disappeared into the guest room. Once inside, I shut the door and leaned my back against it, releasing a shaky breath. I wanted to take a moment to let what just happened sink in, but

I had to slip out of the house and return unnoticed. And thanks to the conversation I'd overheard between him and one of his guards, I knew the security system was still down. Nerves fluttered in my stomach like a swarm of locusts. The blood oath we'd taken was something I took seriously, and what I needed to do wasn't information that would go against that—it wasn't about his family or anything pertinent to mine.

I should have asked Nico to take me to get my stuff, but I had severe trust issues from Dad and Not-Brother. And I couldn't leave another part of Mom behind if he refused to stop and get the bag.

I drew the blinds then went to the dresser and pulled out enough clothes to make a makeshift body. After shoving them under the duvet, I arranged them to resemble myself asleep. The only problem was fooling him that my head was on the pillows. I placed them so it appeared as if I was huddled beneath the blankets with the pillows concealing the top of my head. Thankfully, the end of the bed was facing the door.

I stood back and observed my handiwork. It might pass inspection if he just glanced at the bed. How dim the room was would help. Not wanting to risk him spotting me, I waited another ten minutes then cracked the door open. His voice was faint as he talked on the phone.

Tiptoeing down the hall, I peered around the corner. Nico's back was to me as he stood just beyond the sliding glass doors on the patio. I could hear snippets of his conversation, enough to know he was discussing the wedding. My heart thudded against my rib cage, the adrenaline of sneaking out and the worry over who was on the other end of that call hitting me at once. I pressed my thumb into the small cut on my palm, and the sting of pain served as a welcome reminder of the blood oath we'd taken and the reassurance that he wouldn't give my father a heads-up and put me in harm's way.

Shoes in hand, I moved as quickly and quietly as possible to the front door, unlocked it, then cracked it wide enough to slip outside, thankful the security system was still broken. A soft click behind me from the door closing was the only sound I'd made. Heat surrounded me, and I wished I'd thought ahead to bring a hairband or at least put on a pair of shorts.

I huffed out another breath to ease the hammering of my pulse. It echoed in my ears so loudly that I feared Nico could hear it. I set my shoes down, slipped them on, then took off at a run. The one-bedroom beach bungalow I'd rented for a week was a good two miles away, and by the time I got back, I knew I would be drenched in sweat. As my feet pounded the pavement, my clothes clung to me from the humidity. Traffic was sparse, and I was immensely grateful.

Of course, running was the one thing my father had allowed, assuming I was surrounded by a contingent of guards. But it had helped to keep my body primed and ready for the day I would escape, something I'd known was inevitable unless I wanted to succumb to whatever fate he bestowed on me.

Sweat beaded and rolled down my face, pooling in my bra and slicking my hair to the back of my neck, my cheeks, and my forehead. The moisture in the air elevated my heartbeat—the run was twice as hard as it would have been in cooler weather.

The entire run felt as if someone chased me, but I read the expressions of those I passed to keep my panic at bay. I got weird looks, but no one's eyes strayed behind me. It gave me hope. And when the small house came into view, I increased my pace, desperate to get there, retrieve my stuff, then head back before Nico realized I was gone. I slowed to a jog as I approached, sweeping my gaze over any potential place someone could hide to ambush me.

No one knew or would guess that I was there. I'd paid with cash, used a fake ID of my mom's, and kept a low profile. Besides, I'd only stayed one night before staking out Nico's place, finding the perfect moment to approach him.

Once everything seemed as it should have, I slipped the key from where I'd hidden it beneath a rock and fit it into the lock. As soon as the bolt released, I shoved the door wide and quickly went in. Cool air greeted me in a jolt of relief. I closed and bolted the door behind me. The bungalow was small but luxurious, decorated in earthy tans and browns with crimson accent pillows and throws. It looked the same as when I'd first stepped foot inside. The only thing I'd done there was sleep for an hour or two max and shower. Aside from that, the space remained untouched.

I rushed into the bedroom and retrieved my black backpack. I'd ditched Mom's duffel and put everything into an easy-to-carry bag so I could quickly run if the situation called for it.

Its weight would make it impossible to run back to Nico's place, but I could take a cab. After a quick stop in the bathroom to splash water on my face, I headed out, leaving the key in the kitchen.

Once outside, I had to pause, adjusting to the heavy, damp air. The sun glinted off the sea, rippling before me, inviting me to take a moment and dive under the water. I wished I could've. A day at the beach in weather like that would have been heaven—not a freedom I'd had the pleasure of experiencing, thanks to my father. He'd let me go to spas now and again but only with a contingent of "babysitters," as he called the guards.

Since I wasn't running, I twisted my hair on top of my head, formed a bun, and tied it by threading the end through the wrapped strands. With the slight breeze on my neck, no matter how hot, I felt marginally better.

I headed to one of the large hotels not far from my rented bungalow where I could get a car to drop me a few feet from the driveway leading to Nico's place.

I shifted the heavy backpack, tightening the straps, even though it only increased the heat against my back. As I trudged forward, I couldn't help but remember the light in Nico's eyes when I'd surprised him on the beach.

Rather than take the sidewalk adjacent to the road, I walked along the boardwalk, wanting to blend in, if that was possible, given that I wore a black shirt and white capri pants when everyone else was in bathing suits. Still, I felt more inconspicuous on the beach.

With each step closer to the hotel, I scanned the guests, looking for anyone who shouldn't have been there, not that I expected to come across any others from the Mafia. No one knew I was there, and from Nico's reaction, very few were aware of his being in residence either.

Sand peppered my leg as two kids raced within feet of where I walked, their laughter lightening my mood and drawing my attention to their speedy game of tag. I grinned at one of their moms, waving away her apology. Tearing my gaze from the beachgoers, envying their fun-filled day, I forced myself to study the guests mingling by the hotel's pool.

Twice, I had to pick up my pace. It was hard not to shift to vacation mode with all the people around me enjoying the beach and hotel amenities. I took in the many colorful bathing suits, beach balls, and Frisbees flying through the air until one person caught my eye. He stood out in his black suit amidst the casual attire. My heart kicked into a gallop, and I froze on the boardwalk, praying I hadn't been seen. Slicked-back dark hair, a receding chin, and an instant ick factor were dead giveaways —Guido.

CHAPTER EIGHT

NICO

From a discreet distance, I followed Mia as she left the beachfront bungalow and made her way along the boardwalk. The oversized backpack she wore was a recent addition. The bitter taste of betrayal lingered in my mouth, but I held it back, determined to observe her behavior before making any hasty decisions—like putting a bullet in her forehead.

The thing I couldn't piece together was why she was running now. She'd gotten a promise, a blood oath from me to protect her with my name, a binding union that no one in the Five Families took lightly. Something wasn't adding up, and that was what stayed my hand.

Several beachgoers were between us, providing coverage as I trailed her. I scanned the area in a wide sweep, taking in everyone there and checking for any abnormalities. It wasn't until the hotel's pool that I spotted Guido talking to one of the staff members.

His hair had grown out, and I wanted to laugh, knowing he'd done it to cover up the tattoo on the side of his head we'd forced on him. But his presence wasn't a laughing matter, and my gaze jumped back to Mia.

So that was where she was headed… Everything she'd told must have been bullshit. I ground my teeth, deciding on how long to wait to ambush them, when Mia stiffened, stopping abruptly on the wood planks.

I held back, waiting. *Will she wave him over?*

When she ducked behind a group of people, her chest rising and falling in rapid succession, I could tell she was panicking. She slowly backed away from the hotel, which solidified that Guido's presence was a surprise to her. I shifted to intercept her as she pivoted to flee.

I weaved between people, veering off the boardwalk. Sand spilled into my shoes as I angled myself to reach her. A foot away, her eyes widened in shock when she spotted me. I closed the distance between us, locking my arm around her waist and anchoring her against me as I pulled her across the walkway and toward the nearby beachfront restaurant.

A band played on a small platform in the outside seating area, the singer softly crooning to the accompanying acoustic guitar. The height of the lunch hour neared, and the restaurant was pretty full. Releasing my hold on her hip, I clasped her hand, pulling her behind me while I kept an eye out for Guido in case he'd seen us. So far, he hadn't. Conversation swelled as we made our way around the tables then through the inside of the restaurant, making our exit onto the street.

We didn't talk. Mia's pace matched mine, her grip even tighter. After putting distance between Guido and us, I studied her features. They were taut, the color leached from her cheeks. The way her clothes clung to her and the perspiration that had coated her brow made no change to the fear evident behind the mask she'd erected seconds after I'd intercepted her retreat.

"The car is by the bungalow." It was within sight. She nodded then tugged at my hand as she broke into a jog. I increased my speed. When we were at the black Range Rover, I circled to her side, scanning the street as I opened her door. Before she slid in,

I crowded her, my hand wrapping around her neck. Her pulse fluttered beneath my fingers, and I squeezed just enough so that she knew she was at my mercy. "We're not playing games here, Mia." I increased the pressure, constricting her airway even more, and her hands flew to mine, nails digging in. "I'm not playing around here. Betray me—and it's looking like you were about to—and I'll put a bullet between those pretty eyes of yours."

Another few seconds then I released her. She fell into the passenger seat, not bothering to take off her cumbersome backpack.

I rounded the vehicle and then got into the driver's side. "I'm not even going to address Guido being here." My gaze cut to hers, conveying my dark promise and displeasure with one look. "Why the fuck did you leave?"

She clasped her hands in her lap, raising her chin with false bravado, given how white her fingers were turning in her too-tight grip. "I have a hard time trusting, and I wasn't sure you would agree to stop and get my stuff. I didn't want to leave it behind. And then on the way back, it seemed easier to go to the hotel and catch a ride. I thought I could make it there and back without you knowing I was gone." She pursed her lips, and a beat passed between us. "How did you know?"

"I saw you." She didn't need to know that I had gone to her room with Tylenol, only to find her gone and the bed made to look as if she was in it. The urge to hunt her down had been nearly impossible to resist. If she was a plant and here to fuck with my family... things wouldn't end well for her. But those emotions I caught glimpses of stilled my hand. The tiny sliver inside me that was good wanted to give her a chance to prove herself.

Silence stretched between us. I periodically checked the mirrors for a tail. Once we pulled into the airport, I parked in our jet's hangar. The pilot had the plane fueled and waiting for us. I got out and opened Mia's door, ushering her with a firm grip on her forearm up the rollaway stairs and into the plane. For the short flight, we had only the pilot and copilot aboard.

"Give me the backpack." I towered over her, impatient for her to comply.

"Why?" Her head reared back before she crossed her arms over the straps.

"We have an agreement, and you sneaking out is a betrayal of that. Would you rather I instruct the pilot to go to New York instead of Chicago?"

"It's not like that." Her face paled even more, and she straightened to her full height, which was still only to my shoulders. "I'm not your enemy."

"Prove it. Give me the bag."

She huffed out a breath before slipping her arms from of the straps and passing it to me. My fingers curled around the strap as the pilot announced we were ready to taxi down the runway. Mia sank into a club chair, buckling her seat belt, her gaze on me. I sat opposite her, pulling the bag into my lap. After unzipping the top, I opened it wide. Stacks of bound cash spilled out.

I piled a few bundles on the table between us before going back for the silk bags tied with thin cords. Once they too were on the table, I untied and unrolled them. Necklaces heavy with precious jewels were nestled inside. There were rings, bracelets, and a handwritten note. I plucked it from the small pocket, noting Mia's name on the visible portion. She reached for it, and I batted her hands away, quickly scanning what the note said:

Mia,

I hope that we never have to use the contents in this bag. But it's here if we have to leave our home and hide from the man I married. And now, with recent events, I fear that'll be a necessity. There is so much I wish to share with you. Know you are loved, and I would do anything to keep you safe.

If you are reading this, something happened, and I didn't make it out with you. Don't trust anyone in the family. Take the money, use the IDs, and run far and fast. Never let them find you. If you need to sell any of the jewels, make sure you're able to distance yourself because they will be traceable to the family when you do it.

I can't risk saying more in case you are not the one to find this. I love you more than you'll ever know. Be safe.

Love,
Mom

I relaxed back into my chair, the white-hot anger at her potential betrayal and risk to my family ebbing as she showed me the personal items she was willing to risk so much to retrieve.

At the bottom right-hand corner of the paper, there was a small sketch of a flower.

Several IDs, both for her mom and newer ones with recent pictures of Mia, using aliases, were in the same pocket where the note had been. I flipped through them, noting the photo of her mom, to whom Mia had an uncanny resemblance. I dug through the rest of the contents and found a few clothing items, a wig, sunglasses, colored contacts, and a small cherry jewelry box with the same flower that was on the note and also the necklace she wore.

"My mom gave me that when I was little. I didn't want to leave it behind."

I nodded at her explanation then stuffed everything back inside. Checking the other pockets, I found weapons but nothing alarming. "The IDs?"

"Mom had hers in there. They're expired. They haven't been updated since I was seven, but when I found them, I knew it would be smart to have some made for me too. There was a reason she had a getaway bag. I couldn't ignore the threat she felt. I also felt it since the day after she died."

I studied her, mining for clues that she was lying. Her actions, fleeing before Guido saw her and the way her hand tightened on mine, said the most. "Who else knew you were in Grand Cayman?"

She shook her head. "No one, I swear. It makes no sense that Guido was there." Worrying her lower lip, she paused for a moment. "Do you think he could have been there on business? You have banks there, right?"

"They shouldn't know about our presence on the island. He had to be there because of you."

"But I covered my tracks. There's no way."

There was. I pulled my phone out of my pocket and pressed the contact button for Jace Michaelson, a private investigator I'd met a while back whom I admired and who had all kinds of tech that often came in handy. "Jace, I need that app to locate a tracker."

"Hey, Nico." Noise swelled in the background, and I recognized a few voices. He had several brothers, and they shared the same family loyalty to their wives and among each other that we had, which was part of why I trusted him so implicitly. "I'm sending it to your phone now. Everything good?"

"Yes. Thanks. I'll catch up with you later."

I disconnected then slid my phone back into my pocket. I liked how Jace had no problem keeping things strictly business when needed. He and his entire PI team were professionals. The plane picked up speed, and the sound of the wheels against the runway filled the interior. Then we were airborne. I swallowed a few times, popping my ears as we gained altitude.

"I don't understand. It can't be me that has a tracker. I didn't bring a purse or a phone from home." She swept her hand over the backpack. "That's new, and the stuff inside had been in a locker for years. Nobody knew of its existence."

After accepting the download and activating the tracker app, I stood from my seat and motioned for her to do the same. There was no point in arguing. Guido was there, and that alone was too much of a coincidence.

She complied, standing before me with her distracting lips pressed into a line again. I guided the phone over her left arm in slow passes, then her right. It wasn't until I was over her hip that the app beeped.

"What the hell?" She jerked back, her hand pressing against the spot before running her fingers over the area, feeling for anything out of the ordinary. Anger sparked to life in her violet eyes. "That asshole. He must have put the tracker in the cut I got that morning after he drugged me." She snapped the button and tugged down one side of the waistband of her pants to reveal a large Band-Aid before peeling the edge back to reveal a small, jagged cut with three poorly done stiches.

"I'm assuming your stepbrother, Ricco, did that?"

Her lips pulled back in a sneer. "The one and only."

"You have two options. I can remove it here and now or wait and have my brother do it in Chicago. I vote for that option." Trey would fix the sloppy job Ricco had done without leaving a scar. He could also pinpoint exactly where and how deep it was without having to dig around too much, which is what I would have had to do.

"Your brother, the surgeon?"

"Yes." I sat back down, and after she patted the bandage back in place and refastened her pants, she did the same.

"Okay. I guess I can wait."

I texted Trey and told him when we would be at Marco's home and to meet us there to remove Mia's tracker. Three dots appeared immediately, and I headed off the questions that I knew would be coming with *I'll explain later.*

"I'm sorry," Mia said. She reached across the table and rested her hand atop mine before removing it.

I couldn't help but wonder if she, too, felt the zaps of electricity every time we touched.

"The contents in the bag were important to me. Mostly the jewelry box and the letter."

Not the money or jewels. I was a little surprised—curiosity about what made her tick burned inside me. It had become clear that I was giving her a second chance. That damn nightmare she'd had and the fear I'd seen in her eyes before she'd masked it at Guido's presence solidified my choice. I would protect her. I also wanted to get to know her better. "Why is that?"

Her gaze softened, turning introspective, and she leaned back against the chair. "My mom would play games with me when I was younger. The jewelry box was our secret place to communicate without others overhearing or watching—something just for us. She would leave me trinkets, fortunes, and little notes in the bottom drawer. I would put in a drawing for her, a pressed flower, or anything that I thought was special."

"Didn't your mom pass away when you were young?" I could understand why it meant something to her.

"Yes. I was seven years old. The night before she died, I heard her sneak into my room. I don't know why I did this, but I pretended to be asleep. She put something in the drawer. It wasn't until the next morning that I went to see what it was." Mia pulled the gold chain with a vertical bar from beneath her shirt. "It was as if she knew she wouldn't live past morning. Years later, I found the key and note she'd taped to the bottom of the drawer. She must have added them the night she left the necklace."

"What did the note say?" It was apparent her mother was murdered. My guess was that her husband, Joey Tucci, had done it.

"Just what it would open." She shrugged. "A locker at the train station. The getaway bag was in there, and I decided to keep the jewelry box there, too, because if I ever had to leave suddenly, I wasn't letting go of it."

"What was it like for you without your mom there?" Mia was a barely a blip on our radar. There were very few photographs of her.

My instincts said she wasn't an enemy, but there was too much about her that I didn't know. In a way, I understood why she hadn't confided in me about getting her bag. It held something irreplaceable, and she didn't want to risk its loss. If the alliance between us was to stand a chance in hell, though, we had to establish a baseline of trust. And I needed to learn more about her to anticipate her reactions better. She was still very much a mystery.

"I hadn't realized how much my mom shielded me from the Mafia life until she was gone. After I woke up that morning and found her necklace, I put it on and then hid it under my shirt— just in case my dad decided to take it away. I also learned she'd died. He said it was a heart attack, a blood clot that they hadn't known about that caused it.

"Everything happened so fast. Within a week, she was in the ground, and the captain of our guard had been shot. That wouldn't have impacted me terribly, but everything changed again when my dad married the captain's widow. Things were worse than before because with her came Ricco, my new stepbrother."

"How old was he at the time?" Ricco was on our radar. He was rumored to be cruel but effective, and he had been named Joey's underboss and the successor to the Tucci throne.

"He was nine." She drew in a breath and held my gaze. "I

want to make this work between us. I know running off this morning didn't do me any favors regarding your trust, but I take the oath between us seriously. Because of that, I'll tell you everything."

I raised my brows, curious how far I could push her. "Including the information about the inner workings of your family's trafficking ring?"

She rolled her eyes. "Yeah, no. I already told you that would come after we're married. I need to hold some power in this deal. I can't risk you calling it off."

I'd given her my word, but I would have done the same in her situation.

"When Mom was alive, I often saw the kids in both the Amato and Verretti families," Mia explained. "She liked to get together with the other Mafia wives and socialize with us kids. After she died, I only saw the Verretti boys, Dante, Cal, and Adriano, if their father brought them to a meeting, which wasn't often. I liked them. Guido wasn't someone I wanted to be around, but he and Ricco got along well."

"Not surprising there."

"Exactly. When I complained to my dad about being stuck at home and not playing with other kids or even going to school, he told me my role in this life and how he needed to keep me locked away until the day I was to be married."

The Chicago families were never that extreme. Even Camilla Rossi—who was given to Vic Pavlov, a member of the Russian Bratva, in an arranged marriage—had been able to attend school and have friends.

"Dad kept me under lock and key." Her clenched fist showed her anger. "The guards on my bedroom door were a good thing. I could sleep at night without worrying about some horrid prank Ricco would play on me. That nightmare..." Her gaze dropped then locked on mine. "Ricco snuck into my room when I was fifteen and kidnapped me. He forced alcohol down my throat then dumped me on the roadside near one of the family's clubs. Maybe twenty minutes later, a car pulled up with Ricco, a friend, and two guards. They told my dad that they'd found me there. He thought I'd snuck out and gone clubbing. I was robbing him of his investment. At least that's what he told me."

I couldn't say a word. I didn't trust myself because a part of me cared what had happened, which was a surprise that solidified even more that Joey Tucci and Ricco's days were numbered.

"From that point on, I had guards watching my every move."

"What about school? Didn't you get out of the house for that?"

Her fingers deftly untwisted the hair knotted on top of her head. Once free, it fell around her face in loose waves. "No. I had female tutors until I turned eighteen. Dad wanted to marry me off then, but I begged him to let me go to college. At least I got a few years in, even if it was online, before my dad reneged on that deal."

"And Dante? How does he figure into all this?" I specifically wondered whether Dante had planted the bomb outside the club. *Could she and Dante be working together?*

Her grin chased away the heaviness clinging to her features. "He's a friend. He and his brothers tried to intervene when they were able to, but there wasn't much they could do. Before I left, I told Dante a few things about the sex ring my family ran, and he agreed to help me take it down. I couldn't let it go on. Not after what I saw."

"Did Ricco involve you in anything?"

"No. Not like that. I happened to see him dragging two girls from his car and telling Dad that they were new additions. They were my age or a few years younger. I can't."

I covered her hand with mine. "It won't go on much longer."

"Promise me." Her voice shook.

I ran my thumb over the wound on the inside of her palm. "I already have."

CHAPTER NINE

MIA

Nico's actions continued to align with his words. My pulse had settled back to normal after the earlier conflict in the car, when he'd confronted me about betraying him. Nothing good would have come of going against Nico or the Five Families. It wasn't my endgame. Protection—striking back at what my family was involved in that I couldn't live with—was.

The monster that simmered beneath the surface had risen—the one I needed on my side. While I'd been inwardly terrified in the moment, his reaction had reassured me of what I'd known since the first file on him I'd obsessed over—he was the one who would save me.

I settled into a more comfortable position in the leather chair and tucked my legs beneath me, thankful that we hadn't hit any turbulence. While he placed a call to his brother, Marco, telling him when we would land, I studied him. Dark hair that'd grown a bit too long brushed the white collar of his button-down. His sleeves were rolled up, revealing strong forearms. As he moved, the striated muscles rippled, and I suppressed a telling shiver as my mind wandered to what it would feel like to have his hands explore my body.

He would be my first. My father made sure I was untouched —a lamb to the slaughter of whoever he decided to bind my life to. A spark of rage heated my blood. It was my body and my choice. And as my gaze crawled lazily over Nico's angular jaw and chiseled features, getting caught on the sexy-as-hell grin he wore and that dimple in his left cheek, I reveled in my choice. I was more attracted to him than I would have liked, and it made me feel vulnerable, but I knew that would make my wedding night easier than if my dad married me to someone his age or worse—Guido.

That part of me that I'd locked away from the Mafia world, from my father and stepbrother, longed for a partnership. In our harsh world, I wanted love or what it looked like in the movies. Nico's siblings and many of the Chicago Mafia who were in power had that. And if my father or Ricco had their way, I never would.

I'd taken matters into my own hands and bargained for a marriage to gain protection. It was a business deal, but I wanted more for myself and more for this man who could have killed or tortured me but hadn't. It gave me hope for our future, that we too could have what his siblings had managed. I was all in. And I hoped with my whole heart that he was too.

But that was the dreamer in me. I needed to stay firmly grounded in reality.

We began to descend, alerting me to our impending arrival in Chicago. I peered out one of the jet's windows to see the city in a wash of glowing lights against the dark background of a wintery January evening. My stomach was a flurry of nerves. There was no turning back. I was headed into the den of the Five Families, where I would sink or swim.

Even with the looming inquisition I would willingly walk into, the oath between us and Nico's strength enveloped me and gave me a sense of security. I just hoped it wasn't false. If my stepbrother or Guido had made the promise, I wouldn't have trusted it at all. They didn't abide by the Mafia's code of loyalty. Then again, neither had I—I was betraying my family. But no matter how much that went against the rules of our world, I didn't regret it. I couldn't just sit idly by and allow them to hurt women.

The plane touched down with a gentle bump, and the whirl of the engine filled the cabin. Soon, we were taxiing to a private hangar. Once the door was opened, Nico slung my backpack over his shoulder, picked up a bag he'd brought, and guided me down the stairs and into a waiting black SUV.

I held my head high, letting the emotionless mask I'd cultivated since childhood slip over my face. Nico and I didn't say a word on the ride to the La Rosa boss's home. The silence had grown thick and expectant by the time the vehicle pulled into the long driveway, moved past armed guards, and finally stopped before a beautiful brick mansion with accent stones, turrets, and a balcony with a wrought iron railing off what I assumed was a second-floor bedroom.

It was magnificent and very different from what I'd grown up in. That had been more of a prison, lacking the character this one had in spades. I couldn't squash my curiosity about what it was like inside, wondering whether it would be decorated only for a man's taste. My father's house was done with large leather furniture, dark interiors, and most of the heavy drapes closed at all hours of the day. It reeked of testosterone and money, not comfort. He preferred brandy and cigars, an old-world atmosphere.

When we stopped, Nico got out and opened my door for me. I craned my neck to see where our bags were then shot him a look, alarmed not to have my backpack within my immediate sight.

I touched his side, and his warm brown eyes flared with understanding when he looked down. "Matt," he said to the driver, who had just lifted our bags from the trunk. "I'll take those."

The driver brought them over, and Nico slung them onto his shoulder before his hand settled on the small of my back. As we climbed the three steps leading to the large black front door, it opened. A woman in a burgundy cashmere sweater and black pants stood haloed by the light from a chandelier in the foyer. I took in her slender build, highlighted caramel-colored hair, and kaleidoscopic eyes of blue, green, and gold.

It was impossible not to recognize her as Elena Caruso, who was married to Marco La Rosa. I'd heard stories about her from the guards when they didn't realize I was within earshot. She'd hidden from her family in New Jersey, and no one had been the wiser. She'd been my idol. So many nights, I'd laid in bed and dreamed I could escape my life and live elsewhere without repercussion.

She'd had four glorious years on her own. But nothing gained was without sacrifice. I hadn't remained with my neck stretched across the guillotine. I'd left and made my opportunities.

"El." Nico released me then embraced his sister-in-law in a brief hug before turning to me. "This is Mia Tucci."

"Mia. It's nice to meet you." She waved us in then shut the door.

"It's great to meet you too." I kept my fangirl to a minimum, working hard to maintain the mask on my emotions.

"Where's Marco?" Nico wrapped his arm around my waist, resting his hand against my hip.

"He's finishing up a call. Let's go to the kitchen. You didn't eat, did you?"

She'd addressed me, so I answered for us. "No. There wasn't time."

"That's good. Some of the family are coming over. We'll get food ready. Do you want any wine?"

"Later for me," Nico said. "Will you be okay while I grab Marco?"

He'd asked me but looked at El. She gave a small nod. I didn't bother to respond. What did he think I would do, attempt to kill the person who had given me hope when I'd desperately needed it?

His hand fell away from my hip. "I'll be back in a moment." Then he was gone, and I hated that I felt the loss of his larger-than-life presence. It'd been two days, and I was already growing accustomed to him being a part of my world.

El set two wineglasses on the island in front of us, and as she poured cabernet into them, I glanced around their home. The kitchen was huge and loaded with every imaginable luxury convenience. It opened into a spacious living room. Off to the right was a dining room with a table that could seat an army. The décor was light and airy with a color scheme that gave me a modern, contemporary vibe with inviting furniture, bookcases, and nooks for reading.

The sound of a glass being set on the white-veined marble island snapped my focus back to El. "Thanks." I took a sip, relishing the spicy medley of flavors. Before I could comment on how much I liked her home, a door slammed from the front of the house, followed by voices.

"Hope you're ready for this." El shook her head then climbed onto one of the barstools.

I remained standing, unsure of what to expect. Two women entered. I recognized Sofia, with her long chestnut hair and warm brown eyes that were almost identical to Nico's. The other woman, who had curly dark hair and catlike green eyes, wasn't familiar to me. I was aware of everyone in the families, as it'd been part of my studies, but I couldn't place her. More commotions sounded, and before I could say anything to Sofia, Emiliana entered. She'd married Stefano, boss of the Rossi family.

"Mia Tucci." Sofia grinned, mischief dancing in her eyes. "I hear you're going to marry my brother." She elbowed Emiliana, who smiled in return. "I never thought I'd see the day that Nico got married."

I couldn't imagine why not. He was breathtakingly handsome. Power vibrated around him, drawing stares from men and women alike. And his quiet demeanor only added to his intrigue. El made introductions, and I learned the woman with the curly hair was Hailey, who was engaged to Trey.

My hand instinctively touched my hip at the realization that the Mafia surgeon was here. Hailey smiled and briefly squeezed my arm. "He'll be out in a minute."

I relaxed a tiny bit. "Thanks. I want to get the tracker out and destroyed."

"You didn't know about it?" El tilted her head to the side before passing the bottle to Sofia to pour a few more glasses.

"No." I couldn't blame them for their suspicion. I was from one of the New York families, a borderline enemy. As I started to tell them what happened, two more women, both blondes, entered the kitchen. I knew one of them well—Summer was why I'd ditched my guards during the fake spa days. I'd needed to warn her about the Amato family after overhearing a conversation between Guido and Ricco.

Everyone hugged, and Sofia's hand rested on Summer's stomach. *Is she pregnant?*

I'd learned she'd gotten married to Luc, the boss of the Brambilla family, but not about a baby.

"Hi, Mia." The other blonde addressed me. "I'm Lil. Welcome to the family."

"Not yet." Sofia hip-checked Lil. "We need details. If you're marrying my brother"—her expression hardened, and I realized she could be just as deadly as Nico—"you'll have to fill us in on where your loyalties lie."

I raised an eyebrow then held up my palm to show the

wound across it to ease the discomfort. "I've pledged my loyalty to Nico in a blood oath."

"Yet you're willing to betray your family," El noted. "What's the difference between your oath to Nico and the one to your family?"

I raised my chin, needing them to see my strength and not frustration from being questioned. "My loyalty to my family is six feet under and with my mom. I've never taken an oath to my father or stepbrother. And before you say it, I'm aware of the Mafia code. But in their case, I don't care. I don't owe them anything."

"Harsh." Sofia tapped her glass against Lil's, whose expression flared with something that looked almost like understanding. "But maybe for the best. I haven't heard good things about Joey Tucci or Ricco."

"Everyone hungry?" El pulled open the fridge and transferred two large casserole dishes to the island. Then she took out lettuce and an assortment of vegetables. The cheese was last. "We have lasagnas I can heat up. Just need to make the salad."

"I think we could all eat," Lil said to a chorus of similar responses.

When Lil reached for a glass, a bandage wrapped around her hand snagged my attention. Sofia must have caught me looking because I felt the heat of her stare.

"Lil got scraped up when a bomb went off at one of our clubs. If it hadn't been for Max's quick reflexes—he literally shielded her with his body—the outcome would have been much worse." That same hard glint flashed in her eyes. "Know anything about that?"

I recoiled at the implication. "I—no, why would I?"

"We've heard that you're close with Dante Verretti." El turned the top and bottom ovens on after delivering that little bomb.

"I've known him all my life. I wouldn't say we're that close, but he was going to help me sabotage an operation my family runs."

"Close enough to plant a bomb for him?" Emiliana leaned forward, boxing me in to press my back against the counter.

"Why would I do that?" I pushed back so that we were separated by only an inch, refusing to be intimidated. "I want to get away from my family, stop them from trafficking women. Dante was helping me with that."

"What the hell?" Emiliana's lips pulled back, and horror leached her face of color.

Sofia, Lil, and El crowded around her, wearing similar expressions but not as severe or deadly as Emiliana's. Nico chose that moment to walk in with the rest of the bosses and Trey following close behind.

"What's going on?" Nico's voice cracked through the kitchen like a whip. Then he casually pulled me away from them and to his side.

"Nothing." If those women wanted a fight, I would have to step up. Having Nico run defense for me wouldn't win their respect. I snuck a peek at him out of the corner of my eye as he observed the other women, seeming laid-back. I didn't get the vibe that he was there to defend me. "I mentioned that Dante and I were working together but not to go against or harm anyone in Chicago."

One of the bosses, who had dark-blond hair and eyes that screamed death angled between El and Emiliana. El moved to the side, and he wrapped an arm around Emiliana's waist. It had to have been Stefano, her husband and the boss of the Rossi family. Another man went to Sofia, and I knew by his resemblance to Emiliana that he was her brother, Enzo, and Sofia's husband.

"Explain what you were working with Dante on," Stefano growled.

I summed up what I'd stumbled across—Ricco with the two

girls, telling my father they were meant for the holding cells. How Dante and I had planned to intercept an incoming truck containing several more who had been abducted. That it was supposed to occur the day I'd fled for my life. I had no idea if he'd followed through on the small amount of intel I had passed along. But I recounted what Ricco had done, where I had been held, and how and why I ended up at Nico's place in Grand Cayman.

The only things I held back were the details, such as where the women were held, when the new shipments of girls came in, and the security measures in place.

By the time I finished talking, the fury emanating from everyone in the room had given me hope that I was in a family that was the polar opposite of the one I'd come from. Emiliana convinced me I'd made the right decision. "I'll kill them all," she said with palpable rage.

Nico

I was torn between defending Mia, whom I barely knew, and siding with those of my blood. My family had been through a lot, and we'd done it together. My traitorous heart hurt as I looked between my brothers and their other halves and the rest of our Mafia family.

Stefano had left a bloody trail of bodies when he saved Emiliana from a hellish fate. Luc, a recent addition to the Five Families and the new boss of the Brambilla family, had done the same for his wife, Summer, an outsider who had joined the fold and was expecting a baby in July.

Our generation had endured too much, but it only solidified our bond, including the one with Max, who'd been left for dead but returned to us and fell in love with Lil—he'd helped to unite the families and make them stronger than ever. I'd always thought of Lil as the sweetest of the Mafia princesses among my sister, El, Emiliana, and Marissa, who'd been murdered in college.

I'd never thought I would find the love that my parents, brothers, or Sofia had. But Mia kept surprising me, and I was starting to care for her. I only hoped that it wasn't to the detriment of my family.

After I'd made hasty introductions, even though I was sure she knew on sight who everyone was, we broke apart from the group and followed Trey into the room where he had left his equipment. The tracker in her hip had to come out.

My body felt strung tight and ready to snap—her soft skin beckoned me to run my fingers over it. I found it difficult not to touch her. I rarely acted on impulse, but being around my family and witnessing the fierce love each couple had for one another had stirred the cavernous ache for the same within me. And in a moment of weakness, I gave in and slid my arm around her waist, my fingers nudging under the hem of her shirt to rest against her skin as I led her away from everyone. Beneath my hand, her body stiffened, and a small gasp escaped her lips. A deep sense of satisfaction flooded me—my touch had an effect.

She kept her gaze locked on Trey's back and carried herself with the same confidence and fiery strength that had attracted me from the moment I'd turned to find her on the beach with a gun aimed at my chest. She intrigued me more than any other woman I'd known. But none of them had been able to breach the walls of my heart. I supposed that was why I considered myself an abnormality in our family. I was broken, unable to let a woman inside and experience the same all-consuming love that everyone else had.

Which was why this marriage for protection wasn't an unrealistic endeavor for me. The glitch in my decision was how attracted I was to her. And if we decided to lower our guards and explore the energy that swirled between us, I couldn't help but wonder if she could be the one.

CHAPTER TEN

MIA

The door opened, tearing me from sleep. I jackknifed to sitting, my hand automatically going under my pillow for a weapon and encountering *nothing*. Panic swelled, chasing the remnants of sleep away. Four shadowy forms entered as a light flicked on, blinding me. I sprang from the bed, fists raised and ready to fight.

"Ah, look at you. Thinking you can take on the four of us."

I recognized Sofia's voice before my vision cleared, and I dropped my hands to my sides. But I couldn't get rid of the adrenaline coursing through me as easily. I could wake ready to fight, but words would not come until I had coffee.

"Huh." Em approached, and I closed my eyes and inhaled the heavenly scent of my morning drug as she neared. "I think she's like the rest of us. Can't function without her first cup of coffee."

"Speak for yourself," Lil said with a snort.

"Please." Sofia rolled her eyes. "I've seen you in the morning, and it's not pretty. Your words are nothing but lies. You're a coffee whore. You'd cut me if I tried to keep you from it for too long. Case in point, finals week of our fourth year in college."

"Oh." Lil's laugh floated through the room. "Right. Forgot about that."

I noted it was still dark outside and way too early to be awake. El laughed then plopped onto my bed. I didn't react, didn't say a word, just reached for what Em handed me. My fingers curled around the hot mug, and I inhaled the addictive aromatic scent of roasted beans and caramel. The first sip sang through my body. *So good.* I swore I felt my synapses come alive. I finished half the cup before details in their expressions filtered in, and I remembered what today was.

My wedding.

Sofia went to the walk-in closet of the guest room where I'd stayed and hung a garment bag that I suddenly realized had been dangling from her fingers and slung over her shoulder. I glanced down at my sleep shorts and cami. I hadn't given a moment's thought to what I would wear. It wasn't like the day was about love. It was a business arrangement. I figured we would stand before a priest with a witness or two and be done with it.

"Chop-chop." Sofia clapped her hands, and Em snickered. "We have a wedding to get ready for. And lucky for you, I happened to have a dress in my current collection that would look amazing on you."

Em nudged me toward the huge en suite. "Shower, then we'll get started on your hair. We've only got forty-five minutes, so make it fast." She shut the door behind me, closing me into the solitude of the bathroom by myself. I couldn't understand how there was such little time. Nico had said we would get married early, but I didn't think before the crack of dawn. This was crazy.

With one hand, I turned on the shower, adjusting the temperature. Then I downed the rest of my coffee before stepping under the rainwater showerhead. In under ten minutes, I washed my hair and shaved everything that needed it. I stepped onto the bath mat, quickly dried off, and then wrapped the towel around my head like a turban. A white bathrobe hung on the bathroom door, and I slipped it on, the silk cool against my heated skin.

Then I opened the door, and the girls flooded into the space with me. El leaned a hip against the counter. Em pulled herself up so she could sit on it. Lil was the only one not present.

Sofia pushed me into a chair then got the blow dryer out and started on my hair. El plugged in a curling iron. When Lil returned, another cup of coffee was set in front of me, along with a makeup bag and a spray of tiny white flowers. Her errands done, she settled against the doorframe and watched as Sofia expertly worked on my hair. A sharp pain pierced my heart at all of them in here with me. I'd always wanted a sister, and part of me allowed a sliver of hope that they would accept me and become that.

I wanted to relax in the chair with the soothing feel of the brush's repetitive motion on my hair, but it was such a foreign experience. I had to keep my wits about me. Several minutes later, the hair dryer turned off, and Sofia met my gaze in the mirror.

But it was Emiliana who spoke. "We're here for two reasons. To welcome you to the family and to promise you that if you ever betray us, we will end you without hesitation."

A chill raced over my exposed skin at the steely conviction in her voice. I'd shifted to stare at her when she spoke and saw my potential death in her eyes. I had no doubt she would follow through with her promise. I never wanted to make an enemy of Emiliana.

"We won't bring this up again," Lil said.

I bounced my gaze from one to the next as they issued their warnings.

"And if you ever hurt my brother"—Sofia's expression

turned murderous, setting my pounding heart into overdrive—
"I'll personally make sure you wish for death."

Despite the adrenaline and edge of fear coursing through me from their threats, I fell a little in love with them. I wasn't a stranger to violence, but such unconditional loyalty and protection of their family… I wanted to be a part of that—badly.

Expectancy hung in the air, thick with a tremor of impending violence. It was my turn to speak, and I didn't take their warning lightly. "I chose Nico because of his strength, intelligence, and steadfast loyalty." The fact that he was model-level gorgeous was icing on the cake. And I'd loved his quiet nature from afar, but that wasn't something they needed to know. Nor was the fact that I'd accessed the video feed at a few places to watch him interact with others. "I've already bound myself to him through our oath. I will not betray him"—I met every one of their gazes—"or anyone in the Five Families."

"Well." El grinned. "With that settled, we have work to do. And Christ, these eyes."

Sofia snorted. "Looked in the mirror lately, El?"

I laughed because Sofia was right. El's eyes were mesmerizing. Mine were just… odd. But Mom's had been the same violet hue. We could've passed for sisters if she'd lived. I looked almost exactly as she had at my age.

El kneeled in front of me, and I closed my eyes as she got to work applying makeup while Sofia curled my hair.

"This is sort of a tradition," Lil said from behind El. "Several of us have gotten married before sunrise and in secret. Usually, we get ready at the church."

"Not always." Sofia winked.

"Ha! Right." El plucked a rogue eyebrow hair, a sharp sting following in its wake, while a small smile curved her lips. "Good memories."

"It'll just be us—of course Nico—and Marco, Enzo, Stefano, and Max. Luc wanted Summer to sleep in, so he might be there, but we'll have four bosses present. The capo and Marco are enough," El explained as she finished my makeup with lip liner and a matte deep-crimson lipstick. Then she angled my chair away from the mirror so I couldn't see my reflection.

Stefano was the capo, the boss of all bosses. I could see it too. Emiliana was intimidating in her own right, but her husband was downright terrifying. I respected that, as it was that protectiveness that had drawn me to the Five Families.

Sofia moved back, and Lil took over for her. I felt a few tugs as she separated small sections of my hair then deftly moved her fingers through it with pauses every so often. When she finished, they all stepped back to admire their handiwork. I clasped my hands in my lap so as not to fidget from the weight of their stares.

Then Sofia nodded, a wide grin pushing her features from gorgeous to breathtaking. "She's ready," she announced, leaving only to return with the garment bag. "What size shoe do you wear?"

"Seven and a half." I couldn't take my eyes off the bag as Sofia slid the zipper down. I gasped as she pulled the sides back to reveal what it hid. Tears pricked my eyes.

"No crying!" El fanned my face.

I widened my eyes to keep the gathering mist at bay. Never had I imagined my dress. Or a wedding to whatever troll my father chose that wasn't horrific. It was always a prison sentence in my mind, but they were making real a dream I'd never let myself have.

Almost in a trance, I stood and approached the dress that Sofia hung in front of the garment bag. The fitted white satin bodice featured a plunging V-neck and matching back. The waist was cinched with a one-inch band of the same material, tapered to a tulle A-line skirt. The design was a combination of vintage and modern.

My fingers grazed the soft fabric, and my breath hitched. I'd known she designed clothes and held a coveted spot at Fashion Week in Milan, but to wear one of her wedding dresses… It was unreal. I turned back to thank them and caught a glimpse of myself in the mirror.

"It's gorgeous."

Sofia grinned. "I'm glad you like it."

My dark hair hung in beachy waves. Several tiny braids began at my temple, miniature white roses threaded through them and looped to the back of my head, where they were secured. The makeup application was minimal but effective, as El had highlighted my eyes and lips and drawn a light brush of blush over my cheekbones. I knew I would look like a fairy princess once I donned the dress.

"Do you have any jewelry with you?" El asked, snapping my focus from the mirror to her.

I nodded and reluctantly let my fingers fall away from the dress. I needed a moment to compose myself, anyway. After unzipping my bag and taking out one of the travel jewelry rolls, I sorted through the contents until I found a pair of diamond earrings. They were simple and elegant, exactly right for the day. I would wear my mom's gold bar necklace. I was rarely without it. And that way, she would be there with me in spirit.

While in the walk-in closet, I slipped on lace panties. My fingers ran over the small incision on my hip where Trey had removed the tracker and fixed the hack job that Ricco or whatever doctor he'd had on hand had done. After it was out, Trey had cleaned and glued my skin, and I was overcome with relief. I wanted to be done with my family, but nothing was that easy. And on the heels of its removal, I sensed an impending explosion headed our way.

My father would not let me go without gaining something significant in return. And if he didn't, I doubted he would let me live.

Pushing the dark thoughts aside, I reentered the bedroom.

The girls were a flurry of movement. They had or were in the process of changing. All wore floor-length silk slip dresses with high slits up to midthigh, the deep red the same color as my lipstick.

"Like the color?" Emiliana asked, a strange gleam in her eyes.

"Yes. It's perfect."

"It is. I love wearing this color." Emiliana reapplied her lipstick, her gaze meeting mine in the mirror. "I wear this shade often. It reminds me of bathing in the blood of my enemies." A sinister smile spread across her lips, and I shivered.

Point made.

Sofia snorted. "Only mention what we'll do once," she mumbled then rolled her eyes.

Emiliana straightened and rejoined the rest of us, the moment seemingly forgotten. We had five minutes to get out the door. Sofia helped me with the dress then got to work on making small adjustments with a needle and thread, cinching a few places on the bodice until it fit like it had been created specifically for me.

El left then returned with a pair of strappy nude heels. Warm faux-fur coats were retrieved because it was freezing outside. And then they were rushing me out and into a waiting black SUV.

It was still dark. I had no concept of time as we drove away from the house and to the church. They talked and joked around me while my mind whirled. I knew what I was doing, but I felt detached from my body.

Lil reached over Em and squeezed my arm. "It'll all work out."

I flashed her a shaky smile. "I'm just overwhelmed. The dress, makeup... helping me get ready. Thank you"—emotion clogged my throat—"for everything."

"You're one of us now." Em's dark, serious stare held mine. "We've had the talk, and we won't insult you by reiterating it.

But not all of us had great parents or easy upbringings. Sof and I did. El's upbringing was good but unusual, and Lil had it rough. We understand more than you know."

Her speech was a one-eighty from the dark promise she'd issued earlier, but I understood, refusing to hold grudges. That wasn't what I wanted this day to represent.

The drive wasn't long, and when we pulled up to a church with beautiful stained glass and gothic architecture, El leaned close and whispered that they'd all been married here.

Guards were stationed at the front entrance, and a few intercepted the vehicle then opened the doors and escorted us inside. Marco stood just inside and waited with me while the girls hurried past us.

"Are you ready?" Marco asked.

I met his green gaze with a shaky smile, tucking my hand in the crook of his offered arm. "Yes."

The ornate wooden doors opened, and my breath hitched at the sight before me. I vaguely noted that Sofia was in the position of maid of honor, then Elena, Emiliana, and Lil. And Nico —intense, gorgeous, and soon to be mine—stood at the altar, waiting for me. A shiver of anticipation raced through me. He was breathtakingly handsome in a tux, black shirt, and red tie that matched the color of the girls' dresses.

Between us, filling the nave and along the aisle, were hundreds of glowing candles in all shapes and sizes. An old-world vibe permeated the interior, a window to a time long past.

How did they plan this at a moment's notice?

I clung to Marco's arm as he guided me toward an ancient priest with bushy white eyebrows and a map of wrinkles on his weathered face. Nico turned and locked his gaze on mine, causing everyone else to fade until there was only him.

Marco handed me off to Nico then took his place on the side where the men were lined up. When I faced Nico, my breath caught from the fierce emotion swirling in his eyes, and my heart skipped a beat. I wanted this so badly. Tears filled my eyes, threatening to spill.

He bent and whispered in my ear. "Everything will be okay."

My hands trembled in his. Silence settled, the moment poignant before the priest crooned the words in Italian that bound our lives together.

I felt suspended in time, everyone else fading but the man before me and the firm, unshakable way he held and reassured me since I'd forcefully entered his life. It was surreal, a moment that would live in my mind forever.

We repeated the vows, and Nico slid an eight-carat round diamond set in white gold onto my finger with a matching floating diamond eternity band. There was a flash from a camera, immortalizing the moment.

When it was time to kiss, Nico released my hands then slipped one of his behind my neck, winding the other around my waist and pulling me close. My eyes fluttered closed at the first brush of his lips. Sparks erupted from the feel of his mouth on mine, and I opened for him. Angling his head, he deepened the kiss, tasting and teasing until I pressed tightly to him, my arms wrapping around his neck on their own accord. Too soon, he pulled back. Dazed, I opened my eyes to see his pupils dilated with raw hunger. In his embrace, I shivered in expectation.

I'd asked for more time before we were intimate, but the vows and that kiss had changed everything.

CHAPTER ELEVEN

MIA

With my hand in Nico's, we left the church then got into a waiting SUV. Guards were everywhere. They hadn't taken any chances, especially since that tracker would have led Guido to Chicago. But even though Guido lurked somewhere in the city, I felt protected by Nico's side.

I'd finally taken my life into my own hands and done what was right for me. I glanced at my husband, trying to figure out the best time to tell him I wanted to change an important part of our agreement.

"Where are we going?" He and I were in our car. The others followed in a few SUVs.

"Back to Marco's. We'll have brunch with everyone to celebrate."

I grinned because he'd said it with such ease. Maybe we could find common ground in this arrangement. "And after?"

He took his eyes off the road, and I felt like I couldn't breathe from the intensity of his gaze. "That's up to you. We can stay at Marco's. I'm sure El, Sof, and everyone would like to know you better. Or we can get settled into my parents' house, which is just down the street."

"Is there a third option?" I was having a hard time picturing us staying with his parents.

"They're not there." He chuckled. "I thought it might be more comfortable for you, since the house is similar in size to Marco's. My condo in the city is smaller."

I smiled because it would have been pretty uncomfortable if his parents were in the same place as us. "I don't need a big house."

We pulled into Marco's driveway and stopped near the front door. A few other cars were already there, but I knew they couldn't be anyone from the church because we were the first to leave. Everyone else arrived and parked behind us on the heels of that thought.

"Then we'll stay at the condo." Nico drew my attention back to him.

"Sounds great." The unknown cars bothered me. I was on edge about when my father and Ricco would find out. "Who else is here?"

He winked, and as I was getting out of the car, I stumbled over my foot. Before I could fall, his arms came around me and then pulled me against his body. Heat flooded my face, and I knew I was bright red. His hard biceps under my fingers and his lips so close caused butterflies to take flight in my stomach as the memory of his kiss filled my mind. It had been my first. It was too embarrassing to admit, and thankfully, he didn't seem to notice. I sure as hell wasn't going to tell him that I'd never been kissed at twenty.

His fingers trailed over my cheek, tucking a loose curl behind my ear. I shivered from the thrill of his touch. I wanted more.

"There isn't anyone here from New York, if that's what you're worried about."

The cars. Right. "Thanks."

"Come on." He shifted and wound an arm around my waist,

and we walked past several guards and up the stairs to the front door. "Let's get inside."

I welcomed the rush of warm air when we stepped into the foyer. Nico helped me with my coat as boisterous voices teased my ears. His hand was in mine, and I was holding it tightly before realizing I'd reached for him. It was a shock, but despite how little time we'd spent together, I'd grown to trust him.

My mind whirled with the revelation because it wasn't easy for me to trust anyone. It made my decision about that night feel right.

Something smelled terrific, and my stomach growled. Nico grinned, squeezing my waist, and I laughed.

He chuckled. "I'm hungry too."

We entered the kitchen, where several people were gathered around the island. The petite blonde with the Southern accent was Summer. Her husband, Luc, was at her side. Hailey was also there but not Trey. Two other people whom I hadn't met but knew were also there: Nicole Caruso, who'd been married to the former Caruso boss, Anthony, and their son, Tony.

"Congratulations!"

The shout was loud. Nico's arm remained around my stiff body. Everyone was gathered around what looked like mimosas in the making. Hailey handed one to me first, then Nico. Sofia, Enzo, and the others crowded around, taking flutes already poured and waiting.

Marco cleared his throat, and all the chatter stopped. With a slight pressure from Nico's hand on my hip, we were facing his older brother, who had his flute raised toward us. El stood next to him.

"Welcome to the family, Mia." Marco's deep voice filled the space. "And, Nico, it's about damn time." He winked then slapped his brother on the back.

I drank deeply after the toast. There were so many people

there, and it was such a different experience than I'd ever had. I was overwhelmed but loved every minute of it.

"Mia." Lil's light touch on my arm drew my focus to her. "I wanted to introduce you to my mother-in-law, Nicole, and her son, Tony."

Nico's arm fell away, and he whispered for me to come to the dining table after introductions as I followed her to the other side of the island. Everyone trickled into the other room and began sitting at the oversized table laden with food.

Lil and I stopped in front of a slightly older woman with blond hair that brushed her shoulders, surrounding a beautiful face with very slight laugh lines. Green eyes sparkled as she pulled me in for a hug—a real one. My eyes misted, and I fell a little in love with the charismatic woman. God, I missed Mom. This was the first genuine hug I'd had since she'd died.

"Well, aren't you beautiful? I've got a good feeling about you, Sugar." She drew back and held me at arm's length. "And don't you worry about a thing. We take care of our own."

"I knew it was the right decision to come here. It was Summer's acceptance, how everyone fought for her, that helped me decide to come to Nico."

"It was the right decision." Nicole beamed as she released me to pull a tall, lean man forward. "Mia, this is my handsome son, Tony."

Tony took my hand in his and kissed its back, a mischievous smirk playing on his lips. "It's a pleasure to meet you, Mia."

I withdrew my hand, and he laughed.

"You're not his yet." He turned and went over to the dining room table with a wink, where Nico watched him like a hawk.

Nicole's throaty laugh tore my gaze from Nico. "Stirrin' the pot wasn't a bad idea." She winked and then followed her son.

Lil nudged me. "Come on. Let's go in there and save Tony from Nico's murderous glare."

Brunch was everything I'd never had in a family meal. It was official. I was addicted to the boisterous interaction. I loved everything about the families. And when it was time to leave, because I'd told Nico we needed some time alone rather than staying the rest of the day and night at Marco and El's, I found myself battling nerves.

The drive to his condo wasn't long, nor was the elevator ride to the top floor, which opened into the living room. He owned the building, but his primary living quarters were on the fourth floor. I'd taken note of the guards at the access to the underground parking lot, around the perimeter, and the two stationed at the elevator. It gave me a sense of reassurance. Once inside and in front of the large windows overlooking Lake Michigan, I understood why. The view was incredible.

My visual scan was quick, but I liked what I saw. The décor was flawless and seemed to fit Nico. A black feature wall was across from the kitchen where the TV was. A rug sectioned off the couches and coffee table, creating a more intimate area in the large open space. The kitchen cabinets were black, the counters a stunningly veined white with black.

Nico came to stand beside me, and I acutely felt his presence. It was time we talked.

I turned to face him, and he leaned against the large glass slider that separated us from the balcony and the freezing winter weather. He'd shed his coat and tie. The first two buttons of his shirt were undone. I wanted him to roll up his sleeves. And I was officially procrastinating. A small grin curved his lips, and I couldn't help but wonder what he was thinking.

I'd stalled enough. "I want to renegotiate our terms for this marriage." One of his eyebrows rose, and my heartbeat turned staccato against my ribs. Tangling my fingers in the soft tulle of my wedding dress, I held his gaze while he waited for me to continue. "We agreed to wait to consummate our marriage. And I appreciate that you were willing to go along with my request."

He cupped the side of my face, brushing his thumb over my cheek. "We don't have to do anything you don't want to, Mia. There's no pressure from me, especially since we're just getting to know each other."

His hand fell away, dropping back to his side, where he stuffed it into his pocket.

"Right. We haven't known each other long." I forced myself to stand still rather than pace. "But it feels like more than two days. My father made me study the Five Families in depth from reports he received from his spies or PI on the regular, and because of that, it seems like I've known you most of my life." A nervous laugh slipped out, and my cheeks heated. "That sounds super creepy, but I've spent most of my life sequestered in the house with tutors. Even if only in my imagination, an escape was a necessity."

A deep frown marred his chiseled features. "Your father's methods are antiquated. But I don't view you as 'creepy,' as you phrased it. More a victim of circumstance."

I didn't want his pity, and the brazen part of my personality that my father hated reared its head. "I'm not a victim."

"Poor choice of words." He shook his head. "Forgive me?"

I studied him. There was no condescension, just sincerity. I was overly sensitive. We were getting to know each other, including the quirks we each had and how we handled situations, based on what we'd already encountered. That last part wasn't true—I'd held him at gunpoint and bargained with him, and he'd gotten me out of what could have been a problematic scenario when Guido had tracked me to the island. Then he'd followed through with his end of the deal and married me. Because of those two actions, I'd come to trust him, and I was willing to let him in.

"From what I've said, you know my father's ideas are old-fashioned when it comes to me. And if we don't consummate our vows, he'll find a way to take me back." I pushed out a breath, forcing myself to relax as I held his gaze and conveyed my sincerity. "I want to consummate our marriage. And after"—I cringed, heat flooding my cheeks at having to utter the next part, but it was necessary—"I need you to send him proof."

Only then would I be free of my family.

CHAPTER TWELVE

NICO

Anger rippled through me because Mia felt like she had to prove something to her father. Not only that, but she was likely a virgin, something that was her right to give away when she chose. It was none of his business. I skimmed her features, searching for the truth of her words. But the sincerity of her request was firm in the depth of her eyes and the pout of her full lips. Part of me understood. Abiding by her wishes would set her free and sever her father's final tie to her.

I'd already planned to do that by having a photographer present and getting an additional copy of our marriage license.

I grasped her hand in mine, running my thumb over her soft skin. There was no denying I wanted her, but not until she was ready. Christ, if my sister got wind of the note I planned to send Joey Tucci, she would slice off my balls. Any of the women in our families would, and rightly so. My brothers and I hadn't been raised to treat women like property. Our wives, sisters, and daughters were cherished, revered, and protected.

And Mia, even under the circumstances of our wedding, was my equal. I respected the struggles she'd been through and the fierceness of her demeanor. "While I think it's smart to consummate our marriage, there is no need to do so tonight. When I speak with Joey, there'll be no doubt in his mind that you're mine."

Panic flitted across her face, causing her pupils to dilate. "It's not enough." Her hand squeezed mine. "I can't take a chance that he'll be able to take me back on a technicality."

"Mia." I softened my voice. "I won't let him get to you. Neither will my family—let me rephrase. You are protected not only by me but by the entire Chicago Mafia."

"Thank you, Nico." She visibly relaxed, a small smile curving her lips. "I do feel that. But there's more. I want you. I want this. I want something real between us. At first, I thought an agreement on paper would be enough. But the more I get to know you, the more I know it won't even come close."

"You can take all the time you need to get comfortable with a physical relationship. I'll send him the license and a picture of our ceremony, with Stefano in attendance. That should be enough."

She rose to her toes and raised her chin. I bent to accommodate her height, and she pressed her lips softly to mine. A torrent of desire shot through me at the barest of touches.

She wound her arms around my neck. "I'm sure."

That's all the encouragement I needed before slanting my lips across hers. The press of her body against mine fueled my desire, but I slowed the kiss, addicted to her taste, groaning when she parted so that I could explore her mouth.

***

Mia

My body buzzed with awareness as Nico devoured my lips in a hungry kiss. I pressed against him, reveling in the way he held me tightly. He did nothing more than kiss me, and I could do that with him for hours, but I wanted more, and with a small press of my hand to his chest, he eased back. My eyelids fluttered open, and another jolt of desire coursed through me at the dark promise that swam in his eyes.

I took a step back, and his arms fell away. In the silence of the living room, my heart thudded as I threaded my fingers through his hand. "Where's the bedroom?" I didn't recognize the husky rasp of my voice. He notched his head in the direction of the hallway, never taking his heated gaze off me.

I led the powerful man who'd become my husband into our bedroom in unhurried movements. The room was done in dark grays with accents of steel blue and tan that I barely registered. I released his hand in front of the king-sized bed then turned to face him. My fingers found the hidden zipper on the side of the gown. The sound of the teeth releasing vied with my pounding heart as I eased it down.

The brush of Nico's fingers against my shoulders left a trail of electricity as he guided the gown's straps down my arms until the entire dress slipped off me, the sensation of the silky gown heightening my sensitive skin. The whoosh of air as the garment pooled at my feet gave me goose bumps. I stood before him, wearing only lace panties and heels, then stepped over the dress, inches from him. Heat radiated off his body, tempting me closer.

"You're so beautiful, Mia." His voice was deeper and huskier, and my exposed skin tingled. "Are you sure?"

He'd asked me that more than once, and while I appreciated it, I'd never been more sure of anything in my life. I'd followed his life through reports of the Five Families, and I think I'd fallen for the complex man before me years ago. Meeting him and spending time with him made everything even better because of his words and actions. "Yes, I am positive. I want this. I want you, Nico."

I closed the distance between us, my fingers working the

buttons of his shirt loose, his hands settling on my hips. With his shirt undone, I spread the two halves wide. I explored his well-muscled chest, reveling in his sharp intake of breath, tracing the tattoo on his left pectoral before pressing a kiss to the inked skin.

The touch of his hand as he caressed my waist before guiding me to sit on the edge of the bed sent a volley of tingles through my hypersensitive nerves. He bent, taking my calf in his palm before setting my stiletto on his thigh. He removed one of my heels then the other with deft fingers. His shoes, socks, and pants followed until he stood in black boxer briefs that hugged every inch of his impressive body.

I should've been nervous, especially because of his size. I wasn't. Everything had come about because of the series of choices I'd made. That alone was a heady situation. Being in control of my destiny rather than my father pulling the strings on my tethered will was new to me.

My breath hitched as he slid his arm under my thighs then around my lower back and lifted me against him. Rounding the bed, he placed me in the center, following to lie on his side next to me. He urged me closer, threading his fingers through my hair as his hand cupped the back of my neck, angling my head for his kiss. I melted against him, winding my arms around his neck as his lips brushed mine in a slow back and forth. I moaned from the sensation of skin on skin.

Beneath my fingers, the muscles in his back shifted and bulged, and I reveled in his leashed strength, feeling safe and cherished. He deepened the kiss, his tongue teasing then insistent. With excruciating slowness, his hand moved up the inner side of my thigh, brushing against the edge of my panties, and I quivered with need. Heat pooled, and I squirmed against him.

His mouth left my lips to trail kisses along my neck, and I felt the hard press of his erection as I arched into him. His teeth grazed where my neck met my shoulder, sending a dizzying wave of overwhelming sensations through me. I grazed my hands over his rippling muscles to toy with the waistband of his boxer briefs, tugging until he brushed my fumbling hands aside. Instead, he worked my panties free, guiding them down my legs until I was naked before him.

His hungry gaze devoured my body, and I shivered with desire, exploring the contours of his shoulders as he bent to take my nipple in his mouth. I gasped as he rolled the stiff bud between his lips then gently scraped it with his teeth before his hand cupped the weight of my breast, kneading the sensitive mound. His muscles rolled and bunched as he shifted, hovering over me, then he guided me onto my back, releasing my nipple to trail kisses between the valley of my breasts and across my stomach. Heat rushed through my body, and I clenched my thighs together. I wouldn't survive him. I was sure of that.

Then he raised his head. Desire burned in his eyes as they locked on mine. "Trust me, Mia."

He applied gentle pressure to my legs, and I willingly spread them. I glanced down my body and found him looking up at me, a wicked grin on his face. He ran his tongue through my slit, his teeth stopping to nip at my nub, and I threw my head back, letting out a sound I hadn't known I was capable of making. Heat pooled in the wake of his touch, and I knew one thing—I was hooked. I wanted more of this and more of him. And it was just the beginning.

I writhed against him. When he pushed his tongue inside me, his fingers pressing against my hypersensitive bundle of nerves, I cried out, clamping around him, overwhelmed by the flood of sensations.

The more he feasted, the wetter I became, panting from the waves of desire building to an almost impossible height. I whimpered at the unfamiliar sensation when his tongue vied with his fingers. His caresses changed to urgent, in sync with my escalating need. Then he was moving one, then two fingers deep inside me, hitting something that caused an explosion of stars behind my eyes. I bucked against him, my fingers tangled in his dark hair, as I rode out the orgasm.

When my body went limp, he raised his head, his eyes smoldering and flashing me a wicked grin. His lips were slick and full from tasting me, and I almost went over the edge again. He was so incredibly gorgeous.

He got up to grab a condom from the bedside table's drawer, giving me time to drool over every inch of his sculpted body visually. I didn't linger long on the size of his cock, worried about what would happen when he pushed it inside me.

With the condom on, he settled some of his weight over me. I felt the press of him at my opening, and I sucked in a breath, tensing, but he didn't move, only teased my entrance as he dipped his head to take my lips with his, still coated with my taste.

He deepened the kiss, and I relaxed, running my hands over every inch of him, desperate for more. Then he was pushing into me. Intense pulses shot through my body, and I gripped him as he eased in. I felt stretched to the max. Everything was too tight, and I tensed in anticipation of the pain I knew would come.

Panic crawled through me, and my breath came in short pants. But he didn't push any farther, and slowly, my body adjusted to him. I sighed as his tongue teased mine, and desire built back up until my legs wrapped around his waist. The change in position increased the pressure.

Then with one swift thrust, he breached the membrane. Pain shot through me, and I cried out, my muscles locked.

He held himself still, not moving an inch. "Are you okay?"

I nodded but kept my eyes squeezed shut. When a tear leaked out from the corner, he kissed it away, whispering words of encouragement until I relaxed once more. But he didn't move, and my panic ebbed from his restraint. A sense of joy filled me at the way he took care of me and the knowledge that what we'd just done had been in my control and not something taken from me, which would have happened if I'd never left.

"Mia," his husky voice rasped near my ear, "stay with me."

As the discomfort faded, I realized I had nothing more to worry about. I slowly shifted my hips and moaned. Ripples of pleasure released from my core, making my breath catch in my throat. Nico hummed a low rumble, maintaining his statuesque stillness. My desire for him climbed, and I wanted him to move. My hands rubbed his shoulders, the muscles strong and firm under my touch. I pressed my lips to the same spot where he'd nipped at my skin, and he growled. I grinned, excited to see what I'd just unleashed.

The muscles in his back flexed beneath my fingertips as he moved inside of me, his gaze boring into mine, monitoring my responses. I sighed as desire loosened my tense muscles. He took my lips in a kiss, controlling my body with every touch, every caress, doing things to me I'd only ever fantasized about but never thought I would have.

My body came to life when he thrust deep, and I whimpered as my need for him grew to unchartered heights. Desperate for more, I arched my back beneath him to meet his every move. My body sizzled and hummed from his touch. I writhed beneath him from the buildup of desire as my core shot sensation after sensation through me with each powerful thrust.

Then he slid a hand between us, pressing against my clit, and I cried out. My body convulsed around him, squeezing him tight. He whispered my name as he pushed deep inside me, chasing my orgasm then following with his own.

Shaken, I took his weight as he covered me, and I knew with every fiber of my being that I would never be the same again. Limp and relaxed, I trailed my fingers through his hair.

"How do you feel?"

I grinned as I met his gaze that warred with desire and concern. "Delightfully sore."

He chuckled then pulled out, and I felt the loss of him. After he disposed of the condom, he lay on his back, drawing me close so my head rested on his chest, his arm anchoring me to him.

I floated in a delicious haze of sensations, relaxing against the heat of his body, content in the knowledge of what we'd shared. Whatever came at us next—and I was well aware that would be sooner rather than later—I was no longer alone. We would tackle each adversary as husband and wife.

CHAPTER THIRTEEN

NICO

I stood at the sliding glass doors, overlooking the vastness of the partially frozen lake and cloudy sky, contemplating what our next move should be. Mia and I had spent the remainder of our wedding day relaxing, the one thing I could do for her since a honeymoon wasn't in the cards, given the danger she was in.

I'd drawn us a bath, and we'd soaked in it to ease her soreness, her back resting against my chest. Candles glowed throughout the large en suite while we sipped wine and talked. I'd ordered delivery for dinner, and we spent the rest of the evening cozied up together on the couch.

The only dark spot on the night was earlier, when I'd enclosed a copy of our marriage certificate and a picture of the ceremony with the capo present and had it hand delivered to her father. By then, Joey Tucci would've received the package, along with the handwritten note explaining that Mia was my wife—he no longer had any claim to her.

The next day, I counted the minutes until Joey called. I had to head him off in the best way possible. I'd already contacted my family, and they were headed over.

I was ready for his call and craved the confrontation. I preferred to deal with him myself. Once that happened, we needed to have a plan in place, specifically with all the details Mia had promised to share about infiltrating the Tucci sex ring.

Flurries danced outside the glass panes, soon to blanket the landscape. I loved the snow's freshness and the symbolism of a new start, something I wanted Mia to know she had. It struck me seemingly out of nowhere that if she wanted to finish college in person, I wanted to give her that. Not some online bullshit.

When I heard her bare feet padding down the hallway, I turned. She took my breath away every damn time. She'd left her long black hair down after showering. It only accented her purplish-blue eyes, high cheekbones, and those full lips that I craved to taste. I doubted that I would ever get enough of her, which still shocked me. Maybe it wasn't love yet, but the chemistry, the attraction between us, wasn't something I'd experienced before.

She was of average height, so the top of her head came to my shoulders. She appeared delicate, but I knew she wasn't—no one raised in our world was. The Mafia bred fighters, killers, and sometimes psychopaths. When my sister arrived, I wanted her and the others to work with Mia and assess her fighting skills to see if she could improve. I never wanted her to be vulnerable if I or one of my brothers wasn't there to protect her.

"Morning." Her voice was raspy from sleep.

I grinned and pulled her into my arms, kissing the top of her head as I squeezed her. "Morning. Need some coffee?"

"Desperately," came her muffled reply.

Trailing my hand along her arm, I grasped her fingers and led her to the island, where I fixed a cup for her. Not even a second after I set it down, my phone rang. I glanced at the caller ID, noting a few texts from Trey and Marco, saying they were on their way up, and a pissed-off one from my sister about leaving her out.

It was too early to deal with her ballbusting. I would have to thank Trey for blabbing about coming here because I was sure he had. We were all close, but she and Trey were closest, just as Marco and I were. But I loved my sister and wanted to protect her as much as possible from whatever would happen with the Tucci family, even though it looked like she would be in on our plan too. A part of me swelled with pride at her willingness to aid Mia and do what was right.

The ringing blared through the open space, nearing when it would roll over to voicemail. I winked at Mia's knowing stare. It was her father. I was going to enjoy this. On the fifth ring, I answered. "Nico La Rosa."

"Nico, this is Joey Tucci." His gravely self-assured voice boomed through the speaker. "It seems we have unfinished business to discuss. You married my daughter without my blessing or any negotiation. We can rectify that now, or I will be taking her back."

I laughed. "Go ahead and try. Mia is mine in every way. The marriage is binding, and there will be no negotiation between you and me or my family."

"It's unfortunate you think that, boy."

I snorted, amused that he thought he could put me in my place. He kept tabs on the Chicago Mafia, but he didn't know what I was capable of. "We have nothing to discuss."

"Then it's a war you want. Mia is my daughter."

"She's my wife. You don't have any right to her, and if you try to take her from me, you'll wish for death long before it'll come."

"I have every right!" Joey shouted. "If she isn't delivered to my home by the end of today, I will retaliate."

I couldn't keep from grinning. I relished the confrontation after learning about the isolation Mia suffered. He viewed her as property, not at all as a loving parent should. "War it is." I hung up, uninterested in hearing more.

Mia regarded me with raised eyebrows. "So that went well."

I shook my head, amused. "It went as expected."

The elevator's soft ping sounded, and Mia's head whipped in its direction, her body tense.

"It's family. We need to meet today to address what's next with your father."

I rounded the island to her side as the doors swooshed open, and my sister, Enzo, Trey, Hailey, Marco, and El entered our living room. Understanding flashed in Mia's eyes before she greeted them. It was time she told us everything.

Sofia flung her coat over the back of my couch. "I smell coffee."

"You know where to get it." I shared a smirk with Trey.

Sof tossed her long hair over her shoulder with a flick of her wrist. "What kind of hospitality is that when you drag us here at this ungodly hour?"

"It's nine, not five in the morning, drama queen, and you bought the Nespresso machine, which means you know perfectly well how to use it. And when haven't you helped yourself to whatever you want?"

"Hmm." Sof tilted her head to the side. "Fair."

El and Hailey hung their coats in the closet then joined my sister and Mia in the kitchen while I went into the living room, where my brothers and Enzo had congregated. It gave my sister and the others time to chat with Mia before we got down to business.

I sat on the couch near Trey. "Joey Tucci called this morning."

"Got the package you sent?" Marco asked.

I'd texted him last night about what I would do, per Mia's request. He was all for it. "Since I won't return her to him or offer something in exchange, he's ready to go to war."

Enzo chuckled. "He will have lost a lot more when we're done with him."

Mia, my sister, El, and Hailey joined us, each carrying a coffee mug. Mia settled next to me, our thighs pressed together, distracting me from what needed to happen next.

"That's my cue?" She took a sip of her drink and then set it on the coffee table and threaded our fingers together. "Can I have your phone?"

I handed it over, waiting to see what she would do. She tapped the app for Google Maps then typed in an address before handing it back.

"That's where I was held."

I hit the destination on the map to pull up what I was looking at and studied the surrounding area.

"Every Thursday night, a van drops women off in the alley at the rear door of the club my family owns. An armed guard takes them inside. I don't know how long they are kept there or what's done. The only things I was able to learn were the patterns of the drop-offs and the code to get into the building."

"How many guards?" Marco draped an arm around El.

"From what I could tell, there should be two stationed inside by the exits. On the elevator, I noticed another. But the stairs were oddly unguarded. I don't know if I got lucky and if the person assigned there had left briefly. How many more there are isn't something I have intel on."

I copied the address and sent it and the club's name to everyone in a group chat. "We need to act now if Joey concludes that Mia told us anything we can use against him."

Mia shook her head. "He won't. But Ricco will."

"And Guido is a part of this?" Enzo asked. "How about the rest of the Amato family?"

"It's doubtful." Mia frowned.

"We should have killed Guido when we had the chance." El glared at Marco. "Either time."

"It was Stefano's call," Marco answered, clearly unperturbed. "And Guido is the least of our problems."

"What about Dante Verretti?" Trey tugged Hailey closer to him on the couch then glanced at his phone.

"Somewhere to be?" I was being a dick, but I wanted a plan nailed down.

"I have a surgical follow-up this morning." Trey quirked an eyebrow, his gaze locked on mine.

I was agitated. Too much hung in the balance. I wanted Mia to have peace of mind that she could go out with my sister or any of the others with guards but still feel safe. I refused to do to her what her father had and isolate her.

"Who's going on this little venture?" Sofia interrupted, probably sensing that things needed to move along.

"I propose we don't take everyone. We need one or two bosses to stay back in case we're being watched and our enemy chooses to strike at those left behind. Mainly Summer, Hailey, Lil, and Nicole. Luc and Max could remain here. That would be enough."

"I agree." Marco slapped his open palm on his thigh. "Emiliana won't want to be left out of the ambush."

"We can split into teams," El said. "Mia, Sofia, Emiliana, and I could rescue the women in the holding cells while you guys wipe out the rest."

"I like that plan." Mia grinned.

"I'll go to Stefano's and fill him in. As soon as we have a departure time, I'll update everyone." Marco rose, pulling El to her feet.

Mia and I followed my brothers and sister to the door, saying our goodbyes. Then it was the two of us, and Mia turned to me with excitement shining in her beautiful eyes. I felt it too. It was the beginning of the end of a part of her life and had been a long time coming.

CHAPTER FOURTEEN

NICO

Mia's hand was tight in mine as we hurried from the car to the waiting jet. Evening was fast approaching. Marco had conferred with Stefano, and our plan was a go with a few modifications. Fine by me. What mattered was that it happened soon. And even though I would have preferred that Mia stay back in Chicago, safe and far from the Tucci family, I knew she needed to do this. I would be there every step of the way.

We took precautions not to be followed. Multiple cars had left our condo's underground parking, all going in different directions. When we were sure there wasn't a tail, we'd circled back to the airport and parked in the private hangar. Stairs were already waiting, and we climbed them and entered the jet. The cabin was packed with Trey, Marco, El, Sofia, Enzo, Stefano, and Emiliana. Even Tony, Max's brother, had decided to join us. Another plane contained our captains and guards. We were bringing enough manpower that I hoped nothing would go wrong.

Then we were taxiing down the runway. The sound of the wheels filled the cabin, increasing in volume until we lifted off.

Mia slipped her hand into mine, and I could practically feel the nervous energy radiating off her.

Soon, we would be in New York.

"We're in position." Enzo's voice sounded through my earpiece. He was with my sister and Tom, Marco's captain, who was often in charge of keeping Sofia safe. Once Tom had started dating Nicole Caruso, Gerardo, also present, had stepped up, training to take many of Tom's duties.

One by one, everyone else on our team sounded off with their established locations for our mission to intercept the incoming truck that would bring more women and girls into the prostitution ring. Since Mia didn't know which direction the truck would come from, we'd split up. Each team had five people. Mia, El, and Sofia would be the decoys to get the truck to stop. None of us liked it, but the plan was solid. Next to me, Mia wore a short, sequined club dress, four-inch heels, and a faux fur coat wrapped around her slender frame.

We waited on a sidewalk, pressed against a building with people milling about, not far from a club. The two guards with us and I were in dark clothing, jackets, and hats. We blended into the shadows. Mia, when she shed her coat, would shine. Her hair was styled and sexily mussed. Smoky eye makeup and deep-red lipstick completed her look. For the time being, she was tucked in the shadows with us, wrapped in my embrace to stave off as much of the bitter evening chill as possible.

"There." Mia pointed a gloved finger at a black van half a block away.

She removed her coat and gloves, which I handed to one of the guards. In the long-sleeved, low-cut dress that hugged her curves, Mia stepped into the better lit part of the sidewalk. Wobbling unsteadily, she worked to sell an intoxicated party-girl look. She raised one hand and pushed the hair from her face, ensuring that the guys in the truck would get a good visual. She pivoted, weaving away from the sidewalk and toward the perfect place to get abducted. She purposely bumped into a man, stumbled, then waved her arms, shouting a few words before dismissing him and heading down the alleyway, away from the sidewalk.

Her small scene and solo entry into the alleyway weren't missed. Two minutes later, the van followed. Headlights illuminated Mia in a halo effect. Staying clear of the van's side mirror trajectory, the guards and I slipped into the alleyway. The stench of garbage increased as we went farther. One of the guards went around to my left. He would be the first point of contact.

The truck slowed about a foot from where Mia, seemingly oblivious to the approaching vehicle, swayed her way down the center of the alley. Anger swirled in my gut. This needed to end quickly.

The van's brake lights flashed as it slowed to a stop. Then the passenger side opened, and a man got out without closing the door. Tucci's soldier never searched the area, trusting that it was still empty, staying focused on the prey before him. That was his first mistake.

Mick, the guard who had taken position in front of me, sprinted to the passenger door and launched himself inside. There was a dull thud, and the van rocked from side to side. The soldier who had rounded the front of the van gripped Mia's arm like a vise.

As his gun swung toward her, she yanked out the knife sheathed to her thigh under her fitted dress. I could see the surprise in his eyes as she went from inebriated to alert and fighting in a second. Then he spotted me coming in hot. The angle of his gun rose to block her blade's thrust. My hand clamped on his arm. Applying pressure, I twisted it away from her.

Mia rotated her fist and thwacked the soldier in the temple twice then grabbed his gun and hit him hard in the back of his head. With the last strike, his eyes rolled back in his head. I twisted him with a hard pull, bent my knee, and tossed him over my shoulder in a fireman's carry as his gun clattered to the pavement. Mia bent and swooped it up. Mick met us at the back of the van with the keys. When it was unlocked, he drew the doors wide. Inside, three young women huddled together, fear a beacon in their wide eyes.

I bent and threw the soldier off me. He landed in a loud thud at the girls' feet. "You'll be fine," Mia whispered to the girls, but the terror remained on their faces. Mick made quick work of zip-tying his arms and legs before shutting and locking the back doors.

Our two soldiers climbed into the van's front seat and pulled away, heading to the motel where we would stage the next part of our plan. Once Mia's coat was back around her shivering shoulders, I passed the information that we'd caught them through our communication links to the rest of our teams. With my arm around her waist, we hurried back to the parking garage and our car.

The sidewalks were just as crowded when we rejoined the pedestrians heading home or out for the evening. When we got to the car, I cranked the heat to chase the chill from the bitter winter wind. After the car started, we quickly headed out and onto the busy streets. Mia turned to me at a light, the air crackling with intent.

"I have a confession to make," she whispered, tucking a few strands of midnight hair behind her ear. "It's not the best time to bring this up"—she grinned—"but we have the time."

The way her eyes shone, the cornflower-blue flecks

sparkling like stars in a purple haze, made everything in me sharpen in awareness of what she would say next.

"I've been attracted to you for a while now."

"We've only known one another a handful of days." Even as I said it, I felt the connection that'd formed. There had been an undeniable spark the moment we'd first touched. Some part of me had recognized her as the one even in our standoff on the beach.

She shrugged. "Maybe in the typical sense. You already know that my father required me to study the Five Families. There was something about you that kept pulling me back. He thought you, Trey, and Tony were the least likely to be a threat." She shook her head. "I knew he was wrong about you."

"Did you, now?" I linked her hand with mine, the need to touch her too great to deny.

"Yes. It was the intelligence that shone through your eyes, the calculated decisions… and you have the same unshakable power radiating from you that the other bosses do. My father hadn't noticed how quickly you process things and mistook the quiet aspects of your personality for weakness, not the conviction and strength that they are. I would sneak into his office at three in the morning and search it for any other intel he had on you but wouldn't share with me. I found so many pictures, details about the war with the Russian Bratva, and"—she glanced down, breaking the intimate connection between us—"a few more."

My blood heated at her confession. It sounded like an infatuation and would typically have shut me down to push the woman away. With Mia, everything was different. I had come alive. And a part of me had been more than intrigued with the very few pictures we had of her and how she'd risked so much to warn Summer when she was in danger. "Tell me. What else was there?"

Mia leaned in as we stopped for a light. "It doesn't matter.

Just notes he had. His inaccurate assessment. It'll make him misjudge you in critical moments. I see you. He never has."

Fuck. I threaded my fingers into her hair. Cupping the back of her neck, I drew her to me and crashed my mouth against hers, needing to taste her, consume her. There was nothing like Mia. She was in my blood, and I was never letting her go.

The cars honking pierced through the haze of desire, and I reluctantly broke the kiss. We sped through the streets as quickly as we could in the congested traffic. Her words played through my mind, further convincing me of how fate worked in strange ways. It was something I hadn't fought and wouldn't.

I think she might be the one.

Her confession sealed my train of thought about what we could be. But once Joey Tucci realized Mia was behind tonight's bust, she would have a bounty on her head.

CHAPTER FIFTEEN

NICO

The motel room was far from the route the van would have taken to drop the girls off, but it was perfect for what we had planned. The dated interior and lackluster staff gave us the anonymity we required. It wasn't anywhere the Tucci or Amato family would guess us to be, either, which had its benefits. Mia and I would be seen entering an exclusive hotel in Manhattan shortly.

I glanced at Mia, who crouched and whispered to the terrified girls. Mia, Emiliana, El, and my sister would get as much information from them as possible while we worked on Tucci's guards. Then Enzo, Sofia, Marco, and El would leave for the Tuccis' nightclub, wearing disguises so they could search for where the girls were taken after the holding cells. Stefano and Em were the only ones who would remain in the shadows.

I blocked out what they were doing and focused on the two zip-tied men before me. One was tied to the desk chair, the other secured but sitting on the bed. He was the one Stefano would interrogate. Trey had injected them with his version of truth serum. It wasn't a miracle drug—it wouldn't make them tell the truth, but it would slow the neurological signals throughout their bodies, making it difficult to perform high-function tasks like formulating a lie.

Trey stood back, waiting for the drug to work through their blood. Stefano hovered, malice oozing from his frown and setting the tone for the captured men. Enzo, Tony, and Marco hung back, having agreed that Stefano and I would do the dirty work of bloodying them.

The problem was Emiliana, who had death in her eyes. Neither of us could deny her that right. The final shot would be from her. Just not here.

Trey clapped Stefano on the shoulder then went to a small table set up in the back corner of the room. That was our signal that the men were ready for questioning. I got started on the one secured to the chair.

We were all trained in torture, but Stefano had lived through it due to his father's twisted methods of raising a son he found lacking, never able to view past the façade Stefano wore to see what lay beneath until it was too late.

I blocked most of what was going on around me, needing to focus on my task. The soldier looked to be in his thirties. There was no identification on him or the other guy. They wore dark clothes and were armed—foot soldiers operating on a need-to-know basis.

The sound of Stefano's fist as he hit his guy filled the room. Quiet whimpers from the kidnapped victims vied with our girls' reassurances. I positioned my foot on the front end of the chair's seat, between the guy's legs, and gave it a shove along the dark threadbare commercial-grade carpet until the back hit the desk.

I felt Mia's gaze as I braced myself on the desk, boxing the guy in with my arms. Staring into the soldier's beady brown eyes, I waited for a flicker of emotion. Intimidation was accomplished in many ways. Without the drug, words wouldn't have been necessary at that stage—I would have begun breaking things, starting with his fingers. Then I would dislocate his shoulders and add a few stab wounds before asking the first question. But Trey had done the heavy lifting with the drug, and I wanted answers sooner rather than later.

Stefano preferred to have a little fun before questioning began. A lot of it was for Emiliana's benefit, some kind of atonement for all she'd gone through. I understood and wouldn't begrudge him his rage at the situation.

The stench of fear hung heavily in the air. Even if it was mainly from the abducted girls. I maintained eye contact with my guy, watching for any signs of a lie, which would have been hard but not impossible for him. We were conditioned to withstand such drugs, though I doubted the Tucci family trained their soldiers that well.

"Who do you report to?" I started with an easy one.

"Ricco Tucci."

Interesting. I'd assumed it was Joey. I would get to that soon enough. "What does Ricco task you to do?"

"Find the girls he's targeted, or easy prey, and bring them to the alley behind the club. Drop them off to the other soldiers at the back entrance."

I already knew where and how often, but we needed to ensure there wasn't anything we didn't know. "How often do you pick up the girls?"

"Once a week."

"Are there others who do the same thing as you?"

"Yes." His eyelids were hooded, and he could barely hold my gaze.

We needed to find every arm of the operation. "When?"

"Dunno. We do what we're told. This is the night we go out."

Fuck. We needed to grab someone with access to more of the details, such as the captain of the guard. "Do you get direct orders from Ricco, or is it a captain?"

"Sometimes both."

"Which one mostly?"

"Captain."

"And his name is?"

"Dom."

"Where is Dom tonight?"

"Dunno."

We were going nowhere fast. "How are the girls chosen?"

He tried to shrug.

"Did you have a list tonight, or was it your choice of who to take?"

"We had a list."

"You went after that one." I moved aside so he could focus on Mia, who came forward. "Why?"

"Oh, fuck." His pupils constricted to pinpricks. "That's the boss's daughter."

He hadn't known it was her. "Why did you try to pick her up?"

"Thought she was an easy target."

"What would you have gained by bringing someone in who wasn't on the list of girls to abduct?"

"I want to move up in rank."

Idiot. "Bringing in one more girl wouldn't have done that."

"But it would have made them notice me."

"Where do the girls go after the holding cells?"

"The club."

"Anywhere else?" I was losing patience. The guy knew very little.

"Dunno. I only hear about the club."

I caught Stefano's eye. He gave a barely perceptible nod. He was done too. Sofia, Enzo, El, and Marco took their cue and left after Marco growled in my ear to stay in touch. Stefano lifted his unconscious guy over his shoulder, went through the front door to deposit him in the trunk of his car, then returned for mine. Emiliana followed but not before leaving me with parting words: "Finish this."

They would dispose of the bodies elsewhere, which would buy us more time.

Trey and Tony, along with several of our guards waiting in the cars, set the stage at another motel room, where they would leave the van. The Tucci men sent to investigate would find the van parked in front of a room that looked well used by the foot soldiers entertaining the women they stole. Tony would make sure the girls were returned safely to their families or given money and new clothing and a way out of the city. Then he would join Trey, Stefano, and Emiliana.

It would have to be enough to throw the Tucci family off.

I turned to Mia, my blood heating at her devious grin. "Are you ready?"

"Let's do this."

Already in club attire, we didn't need to stop anywhere before heading to Torrid, the nightclub owned by the Tucci family. It was the part of the evening I didn't like. We had guards infiltrating the club as we drove there, but having Mia in New York was still a risk.

"Don't leave my side no matter what. Even if you have to go to the bathroom, the guards will secure it, and I'll go in there with you."

"Yeah, no." She shook her head, her long dark hair sweeping across her back. "I'm not okay with that. I go in alone."

I smirked. There was no way she would go in there without me. That was one of the easiest places to grab someone, and Lil could attest to it. Too bad she wasn't there to back me up on this little disagreement. Mia was stubborn. I loved that about her. She fit right in with the rest of us.

We had one of our guards drive us, unwilling to deal with

parking for the club. When we pulled up to the entrance, I got out and went around to help Mia, who left her coat on the back seat. With her arm tucked into the crook of my elbow, we bypassed the line of people shivering in the cold, waiting to get in.

The heavy beat of the music blasted through the closed doors, vying with New York's ever-present stench of garbage.

We closed the distance from the curb to the entrance, cutting in front of the people at the head of the line. There were a few protests, but we ignored them, stopping in front of the bouncers. There was no need for me to issue a threat if they didn't recognize me. It was Mia's arena, and I was willing to feed her blossoming confidence.

"Mia Tucci." Her voice rang clear, cutting through the crisp air and hushing anyone in earshot who was dumb enough to complain.

"Ms. Tucci, we weren't expecting you." The bouncer shoved open the door, his eyes wide while his buddy discreetly whispered into his communication device.

With her head held high, and her wedding diamonds sparkling on her finger, she walked beside me and into the club. The muted thump of bass increased to a shout-to-be-heard level and pushed our hearts to align to its rhythm. The interior was hazy, and the strobe lights contrasting with the dark could have provoked a seizure in someone susceptible.

We'd decided beforehand to remain on the lowest of the three levels, opting for a quick escape if needed. Our guards would be stationed throughout, dancing, drinking, and blending with the crowd but always watching.

Weaving through writhing bodies, we joined the mass in our small pocket of space on the dance floor. I rested my hands on her hips as we moved to the beat. While she swayed and moved her hips in a figure eight, arms in the air, I glared at the men around us who took immediate notice. It was also an excuse to be on the lookout for Ricco, who I knew would be there upon hearing Mia was.

Then her arms came down around my neck, and I felt her body press into mine. My focus narrowed to her softness and the way she moved against me. After another quick scan, I slanted my mouth over hers in a hungry kiss because goddamn, she was gorgeous.

Tearing my lips from hers cost me. Sexy hooded eyes gazed into mine, and I felt my heart crack open wider, letting her burrow in—something I'd never done before. But that woman, she was mine. I wanted all of her. When we were apart, thoughts of her drove me to distraction.

I was about to tell her that when movement caught my attention. "Incoming."

Her body stiffened, and she moved to my left side, sliding her arm around my waist and freeing my right hand to pull out my gun if needed. Behind my back, I felt the flat side of the knife she must have slid free from where it was hidden beneath her dress.

We were ready.

The crowd parted, and Ricco stopped in front of us, two soldiers on either side of him. It was the first time he and I had been face-to-face. Cold, calculating eyes met mine after scanning Mia from head to toe, pausing on the diamonds on her left ring finger. There was no surprise, which told me his boss and stepfather, Joey Tucci, had already informed him of the package he'd received and our phone call.

"Why are you here?" Ricco shouted above the techno beat.

"We need a meeting," Mia growled.

That whole scene wasn't what I had in mind. "Let's take this conversation somewhere more private." Hopefully toward the back rooms.

Ricco nodded once, his slicked-back hair not budging from the movement, then said something to one of his guards, who cleared a path. He waved for us to follow. We had soldiers on the balconies above, but there was no way I would have him at either of our backs. We moved to the side, and I stared him down until he grimaced and led the way, the other guard at his back.

He led us to a steel door at the back corner of the club, and we went through to enter a dimly lit hallway. When he turned to the right, we followed. After about ten feet, he unlocked a door that opened to an office with TV screens along one side of the wall, showcasing different areas of the club. The top eight monitors were dark, as was one at the bottom right. Those had to have been for the back rooms where the girls were kept. And possibly for two floors below the club where they kept the abducted women.

I positioned us so that the guards were within sight and our backs were to the wall before giving Mia's hip a gentle squeeze. She wanted to initiate the discussion.

"Have you met my husband?" She flashed Ricco her teeth, not quite in a smile, and I chuckled. "We need a meeting with my father."

"Your father?" Ricco's brows rose.

I stiffened at the dark intent that flashed across his face. *What is this fucker up to?*

"Well, he's not yours. Not by blood."

"No." Ricco knocked the surface of his mahogany desk with his knuckles. "And I deem that a good thing, considering what he did."

"We're not here to play games," I interjected, unwilling to let him get away with whatever he was concocting. "Set up a meeting. You can reach us at the Carlyle Hotel"—an exclusive hotel on the Upper East Side—"when you're ready. We'll tell you where."

Fury contorted Ricco's features until he got himself under control. "That can be arranged. Although I'm not positive it's in Mia's best interest." He shifted his gaze from me to her. "Are you sure you want to meet with the man who had your mother killed?"

CHAPTER SIXTEEN

MIA

Ricco's words were like a jolt of ice water thrown on me. I stood frozen next to Nico. I sensed he wanted to leave whatever nightmare card Ricco was about to play, but I couldn't. Because behind the devious malice he wore like a second skin, there was truth. I'd seen it a handful of times, and its rarity had made an impression. He always employed it for gain, but it was something real nonetheless.

"What the hell are you talking about?"

My nemesis leaned against the desk, his condescending manner firmly in place, and Nico snapped. He moved before I was aware he'd even left my side and wrapped a hand around Ricco's throat. With his other hand, he stripped Ricco of his gun then pointed it at his temple.

"Listen, asshole," Nico growled.

I grabbed the gun from under Nico's suit coat and pointed it at the guards, keeping them back.

"I'm the one you'll have to go through if you want to speak to Mia. And if you even think of crossing her, I'll tear your balls off and force them down your throat. And that's just the beginning.

You'll beg for death, but it won't come. Not until Mia grants it. And even then, I may keep you alive a little longer for the sheer pleasure of making you suffer before ushering you into a nameless grave."

I watched in fascination as Ricco's face turned a mottled red, his eyes bulging as he gasped through his constricted trachea. My heart pounded, and my stomach clenched—not from fear but desire. Seeing Nico defend me and monopolize the situation with such ease made me want to climb him like a tree. It was the hottest thing he could have done for me, and I thought practically everything he did was sexy.

He held Ricco sputtering for air before leaning close with his final warning. "Do we have an understanding?"

Another minute passed before he released Ricco's neck enough for him to wheeze out a strained yes. Then he let him go and stepped back to my side, keeping the gun.

We waited while Ricco got himself under control. There was no mistaking the deep resentment pulsing along his jaw like a twitchy nerve. "She'll want to hear this." He cleared his raw throat. "It's the truth."

"Hurry up." I didn't want to be there any longer than necessary.

"This is what I know happened. Your father ordered mine to kill her. And he did but not until after he took her to the holding cells and had some fun with her first. He didn't cover his tracks well enough. When your father found out what he did, Joey killed my dad. Then Joey decided turnabout was fair play and took my mom as his own."

I couldn't see past the red haze. I flew at him, the gun heavy in my hand but pointed where I wanted it at my asshole not-brother's head. I tried to squeeze the trigger. And when I did, my finger met air. The gun was gone.

Nico's arm wound around my waist in a steel band while I screamed and scratched my nails down Ricco's face. An evil smile curled Ricco's mouth before Nico cracked the butt of the gun against his temple.

We left my not-brother in a heap on the ground, his guards closing in to help their boss as Nico lifted me into his arms, rushing through the hallway. I lost track of what was happening or where we were going as Ricco's words repeated in my mind.

I felt the bite of cold as we left the club. The chaotic thump of music lessened then disappeared when we were in the car. Silence blanketed me, and I pressed my cheek against Nico's chest, listening to the steady beat of his heart as the car pulled away from the curb.

We didn't talk on the drive to the hotel. It would only be us in the room when we got there. Until that time, I needed to mine through what Ricco had said, in search of the truth. A sick sense told me that all of it was accurate because of what I'd seen in the cell Ricco had dumped me in.

Numbness settled into my body, quieting the overwhelming thoughts in my mind. When we pulled up to the hotel, Nico climbed from the car with me in his arms. I let my eyelids flutter closed, uncaring who saw. All that mattered was that he held me. I was so grateful that he'd been there.

I wanted to tell him that I loved him but remained silent. It didn't matter if we hadn't been together that long. He'd given me so much in such a short period. And before that, he'd been the fantasy. I'd never dreamed that he would become a reality for me.

I'd caught a glimpse of the bellhops through slitted lids before closing my eyes again. Nothing mattered. It was a place where secrets were kept for the wealthy, and photographs were not allowed. Hushed voices flitted around us as Nico crossed through the lobby, still carrying me, and the porter called the elevator. When it arrived, he entered. I assumed our guards did, too, but I kept my eyes closed, uncaring.

When the doors opened with a swoosh and we were moving

again, I willed myself from the numbness. I couldn't remain there. Too much was at stake, and I had to talk everything through with Nico.

There was a quiet beep. The door was pushed open. Then we were inside. With a sigh, I opened my eyes and lifted my head. The décor hit me first. The rooms were apartment style, classically traditional, opulent in the vintage-style furnishings and luxurious touches.

Nico lowered me onto a white rolled-arm couch then sat opposite me on a coffee table that looked too delicate to hold his weight. He set both guns down before taking my hands in his. "Are you all right?"

"Yes. No." I threw my hands up before standing. I needed to move. Nico switched to sitting on the couch while I paced.

"Do you think he's lying?" His deep voice penetrated my confusion.

I kept my focus on him and his voice, which pulled me back to reality. "No. I've studied him over the years and know the few times he's been truthful. That was one of them. And only because he knew it would cause maximum pain." That asshole. "The more I think about it, the more things stand out."

"Such as?"

He was the calm to my storm, and I grasped on to him, falling to the cushions beside him and pressing my leg against his, needing the tether of his touch. "The flower."

"What flower?" He lifted me to his lap so that my back rested against both his arm and the couch.

I turned my head slightly so that our gazes collided then lifted my necklace and pointed to the tiny chamomile flower engraved into the lower portion of the gold bar. "This one. When Ricco dumped me in the holding cell before I escaped, I noticed a sketch of the same flower where the doorjamb meets the wall. It's in a place that wouldn't be spotted when the door was opened. It had to be from her."

"You think he locked you in the same room where his father raped her?" His lips pulled back in a sneer.

Bile climbed my throat, and I had to swallow the excess saliva several times before I could answer him. I was equally if not more appalled. "Yes. My jewelry box has the same flower. I think it's a message for me."

"But for you to see the one in the basement, she would have suspected you would be there too at some point."

I shivered from the wrongness of it all. "I hope that wasn't what she thought. It's a terrible fear to think your daughter will suffer the same fate and not be able to do anything about it."

"Perhaps she thought you would find out about what your father was doing to the others and try to stop him, not that you would be murdered there too."

I liked that theory much better and snuggled into him, feeling drained from everything I'd learned. "I want to kill him."

"Who? Ricco? Or your father?"

"Both." I only hoped that I would get the chance to see it through.

I awoke suddenly in the plush hotel bed, sensing that Nico wasn't by my side. My hand slid along the soft sheets, encountering warmth where he must have been only seconds before. Low voices traveled through the suite's partially closed bedroom door. A glance at the clock's glowing blue numbers told me it was three in the morning, the perfect time to conduct anything suspect.

After slipping on the satin robe that I'd left on the chaise lounge at the end of the bed, I quietly grabbed the gun from the nightstand and crept to the door leading to the main room.

The closer I got, the more I recognized the voices, and a sense of relief swept over me as I opened the door fully.

Everyone was gathered in the larger living area, filling all the available seats.

Emiliana smirked. "I told you she'd wake up. Come on." She waved me over. "We're finalizing the details for tomorrow."

"Without me?" I glared at Nico, who wrapped his arm around me as I stormed by with a huff. He tugged me into his lap, pressed a kiss to my lips, then grinned.

"I didn't want to wake you after everything that happened last night."

Last night? Oh, right. It was technically morning, even if the sun hadn't yet risen. I relaxed into his hold because he wasn't wrong. The bomb that Ricco had dropped on me had been a shock, and sleep had done me good. "What did I miss?"

"Everything, girl. You slept through the first hour of us talking." Sofia snorted at Nico's glare. She raised her palms in defense. "I told you to wake her up. Before I forget." She reached down and tossed me a pair of black pants.

"Thanks?" I wasn't sure why she was giving them to me. I held them up. They looked fitted, and I took note of the pockets.

"We all have them. Well"—she grinned—"the girls, anyway. There are weapons hidden in the seams and other spots that should get by most searches. They're a necessity, and I thought you should have a pair, too, so I made them."

I laughed, delighted at another weapon to add to my arsenal. They reminded me of my stilettos with the blade hidden in the heel. "I love them. Thank you."

"I'll show you where everything is later, but you should wear them tomorrow. The rest of us are."

I loved them all even more.

"Back to the plans," El said from her spot next to Marco on the couch, where Nico and I had sat when I put the pieces of how Mom died together. "We decided on the location for the meeting this morning. Your father agreed to ten in the morning. We set a meeting point—"

"But that'll change ten minutes before," Nico said then caught the small decorative pillow El had launched at him for interrupting her. "We'll have the area surrounded and will be able to detain his backup as he moves locations."

"So everything's set?" I was still angry at what I'd learned about my father. It was time to confront him. "It's still just Nico and me at the meeting?"

Stefano spoke up. "Yes, so long as nothing goes wrong."

His words cast a shadow over everyone. Things rarely went as planned.

CHAPTER SEVENTEEN

NICO

Light pierced the small slit where the curtains parted, spilling across the bed where Mia and I had fallen asleep for a few more hours after everyone left. We had a day or two before we needed to get out of New York and back to Chicago. If I was honest, staying more than one day would be pressing our luck. Too many things could go wrong.

Dante had called Stefano, saying he'd caught wind that Mia was with me and that he wanted to help in any way he could. Stefano, Trey, Enzo, and Tony had tried to take him up on his offer of help. At the very least, he'd wanted to send his brothers, Cal and Adriano. But Marco and I had protested against adding the additional men, and Stefano had gone along with us.

Mia trusted them, but I preferred to rely only on our family. Since we were here confronting her father at my request, Marco and Stefano—despite being the capo and having the final say— agreed it was my call.

I glanced at the clock. We needed to be out the door in an hour. The key was to leave minutes before we were due at the designated location because of the soldiers Joey undoubtedly had watching the hotel. We'd set the meeting place elsewhere and would change it to the bridge spanning across the lake in Central Park instead.

My gaze fell to Mia, and I drank in how peaceful she appeared while asleep. I wanted her to have these last few minutes of rest, but the need to touch her was too great. I trailed my fingers along her cheek to tuck her hair behind her ear. Her skin was so soft. When her eyelids fluttered open, revealing her unusual purple irises, I bent and grazed my lips over hers, and her eyelids closed once more.

With a hand on her hip, I urged her closer, and when she wrapped her arms around my waist and I felt the soft press of her body along mine, desire raged through me. Lifting her leg, I wrapped it around my hip, pressing into her, and broke the kiss. "You drive me crazy, Mia."

She arched against me then tugged my hair until we were a centimeter apart. "Then do something about it."

My restraint evaporated as I flipped her so that she lay beneath me. The breathy laugh that escaped her full lips taunted me to taste her again. I kissed her deeply as I ran a hand up the smoothness of her thigh.

Every caress we shared strengthened the invisible cord I felt between us. As we moved in sync and drowning in sensation, I knew just how much she meant to me and that I could never let her go.

I pressed a kiss to Mia's temple then slipped my arm around her waist as we walked together from the hotel and into the waiting car. We'd needed that shared stolen hour. After, we rushed to get ready in time.

My gaze traveled over her, taking in the tight black pants

from my sister and a short down winter coat with a faux fur-lined hat and matching gloves. She looked incredible, and all I wanted to do was take her back to our room and lose myself in her all over again.

But we had pressing matters to take care of, and when it was over, we would spend the day in bed with no interruptions.

With the call made to change the location to sputtering protests from her father, we were well on our way to putting an end to his reign of terror.

As we met Joey Tucci, a club raid would be in progress. Stefano, Emiliana, Marco, and El were already en route to free the women held in the back rooms of Torrid's ground floor. It was a risk, but knowing Joey's ego, he would want most of his guards with him. Whether that left Ricco to keep an eye on the club or not wasn't something we would know until the time came.

Mia's gloved hand found mine, and I turned to her. "Are you ready for this?"

"More than ever," she said almost in a growl.

I couldn't blame her. After today, it was my sincere hope that she would be free of the Tucci family and all they had taken from her. She sat next to me, her body stiff as she gazed out the window at the wintery landscape. It'd snowed overnight, blanketing the city in an unspoiled cloud of white. It wouldn't last. Vehicles splashed through the streets, spreading the slush. That wasn't the case in Central Park. Our car pulled up, and we got out to a winter wonderland of beauty.

"Is everyone in place?"

There was a hint of worry in her voice, and I didn't like it. "Yes. They've been here for the past hour, making sure no one we aren't okay with gets in. Joey should be here a few minutes after we're on the bridge."

I tucked her hand into the crook of my arm as we strolled

along the picturesque trail through the park and toward the lake. Even though guards were stationed everywhere, watching for trouble, we both scanned the landscape to make sure there were no surprises.

"Where do you want to go on a honeymoon?" We had time, and I wanted to ease her nerves.

"We're going on one?"

I laughed at the shock in her voice. "Of course. As soon as all this is settled, we can get away for a week."

Her death grip on my bicep eased. "I've only been here, Chicago, and Grand Cayman. I'm not sure where I would want to go." She sank her teeth into her bottom lip for a second. "Maybe Italy? It's hard to believe I've never been there, being Mafia and all."

Snow crunched beneath our shoes as we followed the bend of the walkway to the footbridge. "That's where we'll go, then. My sister has a place we can stay at. And if you like it, as many of us do, we'll look into getting property there." She flashed me a smile that held pure joy, and I wanted to do whatever it took for her to be happy like she was at that moment.

I was about to tell her more about Italy when I caught movement in the corner of my eye. I pulled her closer and slid my other hand into my partially zipped coat to withdraw the gun from my shoulder holster.

I kept the 9mm at my side as we moved to the bridge's center then stopped. The boss of the Tucci family stalked forward, a handful of guards surrounding him. As they neared the entrance to the footbridge, several of our soldiers appeared from their hiding places to detain the Tucci soldiers.

"I said alone." My voice boomed across the space.

Joey snorted, a sneer pulling his slightly sagging features taut. "Yet you brought soldiers with you too."

I said nothing, waiting for him to close the distance between us. As he neared, I noticed he'd stayed in shape. I wouldn't underestimate him, despite his advanced age. With added years only came experience. He wore a trim beard spiked with gray and a black beanie. He stopped a foot away from us, sizing me up. I searched, but there wasn't anything in his features that resembled Mia's. She'd said she took after her mother.

"If you've come to return my daughter, you still owe me something." He wouldn't even glance in her direction.

"We've already been over this. I'm here to deliver a message once more, but this time in person. Mia is my wife. You have no right to her." He opened his mouth to speak, but I held up a hand to stop him. "She has something to say to you. After that, you won't hear from her again. And if you try to contact her, you'll answer to me."

"You're just a pup. No real power."

I didn't rise to his bait. He wasn't worth it. And ignoring him would further enrage him.

I felt rather than saw Mia bristle beside me at the way her father was behaving, but it didn't concern me. What did was that he had yet to look at her. It didn't stop her from delivering her message.

"How could you?" Her voice shook with barely suppressed rage. "You killed Mom—why?"

Joey's silence only fueled Mia's temper.

"Ricco told me all about how you ordered the captain of the guard, his father, to kill my mother."

That got Joey's attention, and he whipped his gaze to her. "Shut your mouth about things you know nothing about."

I launched my fist at his face. The satisfying crack and jerk of his head proved I'd found my mark. As he swiveled toward us, I was ready, my gun already trained on him just as he raised his. We were at a draw, or so it seemed. Blood trickled from the cut on his swelling lip, but he paid it no attention.

"Do not speak to my wife with such disrespect. Her position is greater than yours."

"Bullshit. She's nothing. The wife of an underboss, one who'll probably remain a second for the whole of his life."

"You're a fool. An underboss in the Chicago Mafia trumps a New York boss. I could kill you here and now without repercussion, whereas you would answer to the Five Families and, if a commission is called, Italian royalty as well."

Red infused Joey's cheeks. We'd anticipated his next move. As he shifted the barrel of his gun to Mia, seven red laser dots appeared from our soldiers' guns—six divided to target his forehead and chest. But it was the seventh one, aimed at his eye, that got his notice.

"Do you think I would underestimate you?" I tilted my head, studying him. He was desperate. Mia was his prized possession after he'd killed his wife, and I knew he'd thought he would cash in on her beauty and presumed innocence to the highest bidder to increase his power tenfold. But no one in the Mafia was innocent. And Mia was stubborn and highly intelligent, which was a deadly combination against someone like Joey.

"What'll you do now, Father? You have no claim to me, and Ricco outed your secret—the murder of my mother. Is there anyone you can trust?"

Joey clamped his lips together, and instead, he turned to me, dismissing her by action if not words. "This isn't finished."

"It is."

I jerked Mia to my other side, away from the potential trajectory of his bullet if he was able to fire it. He didn't get the chance. Instead, a shot rang out from one of my men, and a hole appeared in the center of Joey's hand. The gun fell from his useless grasp as he cried out in pain.

"Let that serve as the one and only warning you'll ever get. *Never* point a gun at my wife." With that promise, I led Mia off the bridge.

Her laughter filled the air and my heart. This sound, so full with joy and freedom, was why I'd gone to all the trouble of meeting with Joey Tucci. I drew her close as we strolled through the park until we were ready to go back to the hotel.

We weren't finished with our plan, not even a little bit.

CHAPTER EIGHTEEN

NICO

Mia and I pulled up to a hotel far from Central Park but close to the building where the Tucci soldiers held the abducted women. She hadn't said much after the shit show with her father, and I couldn't blame her. The way he treated her still made my blood boil. When we exited the car, guards following, I kissed her temple and drew her close as we hurried through the lobby and to the rooms that one of the men had secured. I glanced at my watch before quickening our pace. The rest of the guys would be calling any minute, and I preferred we were someplace private when they did.

The room was on the first floor, so we took the stairs. I pressed a camera the size of a fly to the top of the doorjamb of the stairwell. I put another atop our door to view anyone who stood in the hallway. Both cameras would connect to my phone and eliminate the element of surprise if we were followed.

After we were inside, I pulled her into my arms and kissed her. She matched my urgency. I couldn't get enough of her. She was beautiful both inside and out, and I wanted her—always. Not one second of a day passed when I wasn't itching to run my hands over her soft skin, my thumb on her plump lips, or to feel her slender body in my arms, safe and warm.

The sound of my phone ringing broke us apart. I gazed at her while pulling it from my pocket. Her face was flushed, her full lips parted, enticing me to taste her again. I had to force myself to take a step back from temptation as I hit the button to answer.

Marco's voice came through the speaker, further dousing the moment between Mia and me. "Everyone is out."

"No problems?" We kept the conversation cryptic on the off chance that someone was listening. Our lines were secure. We owned a cellular company, and Trey's wife, Hailey, had taken over monitoring it to ensure that. But there could have been bugs in the room or someone listening wherever Marco was. It wasn't worth the risk.

"None. We're on our way to you after a quick stop."

I said goodbye then hung up, and Mia went over to one of the barstools. I took in her stormy expression, wishing I could ease her turmoil. "How are you doing?"

She shoved her dark hair back from her face. "I'm fine." Her hand fell to her lap, and she raised her chin to meet my gaze. "It's weird. I've always known he wasn't a good father, but that altercation and what Ricco told me destroyed any positive feelings I might have had left." Her eyes hardened, and her fighting spirit burned in their depths. "I want him dead. Not only him but Ricco too."

"That can be arranged."

She flashed a humorless smile. "Good. Let's make it happen."

My focus sharpened as she tapped a finger on her thigh. "What are you thinking about?"

"We need to bring Dante and his brothers into this."

"No." I didn't like the coincidences of late. "It's too much of a risk. Our family is enough."

"If Ricco brings in Guido and anyone loyal to him, which I

know he will, it wouldn't hurt to have more with us who can fight." She paused, her teeth momentarily sinking into her bottom lip, and my senses went on alert. "There's something you should know. I gave Dante the codes to my father's house and the guards' rotation schedule."

"Why?" *What is her connection to the Verretti family?*

"We were going to help the women Ricco was trafficking, and I couldn't shake this feeling that something would happen to me. I gave him the intel so he could break me out of the house if needed. But I wasn't detained there, and I left in a rush before I could tell him I was free." She shrugged, a flash of worry creasing her smooth forehead. "I don't know if he went looking for me or not, and I want to talk to him or his brothers."

My muscles grew taut, and I had to work not to clench my fists. "What are they to you?"

Her brows scrunched, and she pursed her lips. "What do you mean? I've known them forever."

I clenched my teeth, waiting for her to answer the question.

Then she straightened in the chair, her eyes wide. "Oh, you mean romantically?" She scoffed before resting her palm on my chest. "There has never been anything between me or the Verretti boys. They're more like cousins." Her finger stabbed my chest. "And you know that from our first time together."

I curled my hand around her finger, removing it from jabbing me, then pressed a kiss to her hand. Pulling her to her feet, I wrapped my arms around her. I had never been the jealous type, but with Mia, all the control I had over my responses went to hell. "We have to talk to Stefano and Marco. The decision was not to involve them. If they agree, you can call Dante."

When I released her, it was to order room service. Everyone would be there soon, and we needed to eat while figuring out who would go where tonight. If our attack was successful, it would be our last few hours here, and then we would head back to Chicago. I was more than ready for that. The Verretti family could deal with the fallout and monitor the actions of the Amato and Tucci families.

I looked around the hotel room, noticing the décor for the first time, and laughed. "Very different from where we stayed last night."

Mia giggled. "Have to say I prefer the other place. This modern lime-green geometric design they've got going would be hell on a hangover."

"We'll only be here until midnight." I decided to text Marco and Stefano about the Verretti brothers. The entire trip had been for Mia, and if she trusted them, I would try to give them the benefit of the doubt, even if reluctantly. It helped that several of the Chicago bosses were okay with Dante. Marco and I had yet to come around, but I hoped that would change after this.

There was a soft knock on the door, and I pulled my gun but pointed it at the ground, motioning for Mia to get behind me. A quick check on my phone to view both angles from the camera revealed that it was room service. There was no one else in the hallway other than two employees and carts full of covered dishes.

I opened the door, still cautious. The carts were wheeled in, and I dismissed the staff before they could unload the food, handing them each a large tip before shutting and locking the door. Mia and I had just moved the food to the small island and the table in the space where the kitchen met the living room when a text from Marco came through.

I winced as I read his message but tried to play it off. I slipped my phone back into my pocket, a sense of dread strangling the words I had to force myself to say. "You can call Dante." It was the right thing to do if she and I were to continue to build trust. And I wanted that, especially after witnessing how her family treated her. "Tell them to get here tonight, and we'll fill them in on what's going on."

Mia slid her arms around my waist, her chin angled high and her gazed locked on mine. I read the sincerity in her expression. "I promise they'll help us. Adriano is a sharpshooter, besides being an assassin," she said.

We were well informed about the Verretti brothers. I encircled her in my arms, letting her fill me in on the off chance there was something I didn't know.

"I'm sure you have intel on Dante. But what you might not know is that he's always been kind to me. All of them have been. Cal is the most confrontational, the only one who would tease me to get a reaction."

"It's fine, Mia. Go ahead and call them." It was better to get it over with. Once they were there, I could judge them for myself.

"Great." She sat on the couch, phone in hand. "When are Sofia and everyone getting here?"

I shrugged. Probably soon, but that wasn't something I wanted Dante to know about. "They didn't give an exact time."

Her eyes narrowed, but she didn't say anything. Instead, she pressed a series of numbers she knew by heart and waited for someone to answer. Then she surprised me and held the phone out in her hand, the speaker button activated.

I recognized Dante's gruff voice when he answered. A relieved smile flittered across Mia's face, and my heart skipped a beat at the sight.

"Hey, Dante. It's Mia."

"Where are you? Are you okay?" His voice whipped through the speaker. "I'll come get you."

"I'm fine. Promise."

"I went in after you missed our meeting." Worry laced his words, making them sound even rougher.

Her shoulders slumped. "I'm sorry. I am. But Ricco ambushed me when I was on my way out. I got away, but I was on the run, and it slipped my mind to let you know I was safe. It's my fault."

I grunted my displeasure at her taking the blame for doing what was necessary to stay alive. Her gaze whipped to me.

"Who the fuck is there, Mia?"

"My husband, Nico La Rosa."

I grinned because while Joey Tucci pretended not to know who had more power, Dante wouldn't make the same mistake. The night had gotten infinitely more interesting.

Mia

Our hotel room had grown crowded. I stood near Sofia, Emiliana, and El, acting as the buffer between the Verretti brothers and Nico and Marco. The rest of the Chicago guys didn't seem to have an issue. But mistrust shone in my husband's eyes, reflecting the same in the boss of the La Rosa family's.

I studied the Verretti men from Nico's viewpoint, not my familiarity. Dante was a beast of a man, all tats and muscles in a powerful body that radiated violence. His eyes saw too much, something about which I knew Nico was more than aware. And while Cal paid Nico little heed, Dante and Adriano made it known that they were aware of both his and Marco's mistrust by the way they unflinchingly stared back.

But I trusted them with my life. They'd attempted to intervene often against my father. The only time they'd let me down was with the arranged marriage. I was glad they'd declined to help, though, because I'd ended up with the man of my dreams.

A small smile curved my lips. I must have made a noise because Nico's focus shifted to me. I felt myself soften just from one look before he tugged me to him. Dante stiffened in the corner of my eye, but I laughed at the rush of rightness that filled me from the simple touch of Nico's hand in mine.

"What the hell, man?" Enzo shifted in front of us. "You're going to leave my wife next to the eye candy?" He tsked before pulling a giggling Sofia into his arms.

"Aw, Enz, you know you're the only eye candy I want."

Trey made a gagging sound and shielded his eyes as his sister draped herself over her husband. "Seriously, Sof?"

Adriano chuckled, dropping his head and attempting to mask the smile that made women drop their panties on sight. I knew the power behind it, but he'd never had any effect on me.

With the tension broken, we got down to business. Dante and I shared every bit of intel we had on the building, Dante brought out blueprints he'd managed to get ahold of, and we finalized the plan.

Anticipation buzzed along my skin at what we were about to do. We were at the beginning of the end of my family's long reign of terror.

CHAPTER NINETEEN

MIA

Tensions were high, and I felt the abundance of power as heavy static weighed down the cold air. Under a full moon, Nico, the others from the Chicago Mafia, and the Verretti family surrounded the back of Torrid, the club where my former family—I refused to think of the Tucci line as mine —kept the women two floors below where I'd been held.

The front entrance had a line of people waiting to get in, as the club closed in the early hours of the morning. Scantily clad women in four-inch heels and dresses that barely covered their asses shivered as a bouncer swept the line now and then, choosing the lucky few, and mostly women, who were allowed into the already at-maximum-capacity club. Loud techno music thumped and bled from the door opening and closing at the front of the building, mixing with people talking and laughing. The commotion aided our arrival and positioning. This was also the time where the hidden floors were busiest. It was the perfect opportunity to strike for optimal damage.

Since Tony wasn't viewed as a threat by my father or Ricco, he stood the best chance of not raising the alarm. The guards would think they could handle him and not immediately inform

Joey or Ricco, which could lead to repercussions if it was an easily fixable problem. I knew them well.

Dom, the captain of the guards, on the other hand, would be a huge issue. He terrified me. An ex-boxer, the man was mammoth with muscle stacked on muscle. His intimidating persona was complete with cauliflower ears impossible not to fixate on, just like a bad car crash. I hoped that he wouldn't be there. It was likely that he was at least somewhere inside the club.

We had SUVs that contained our small army parked everywhere, complete with soldiers and enough room to transport whoever was inside. My stomach rolled at the thought of going back into the basement, especially the room where both my mom and I had been placed.

I wanted revenge.

Nico and I shared a look. He gave me a small nod. It seemed like a lifetime ago when I'd told him that I saw the real him, who he really was. And with that one intense acknowledgment, I knew he was conveying the same thing. My nerves dissipated—his conviction and unconditional support soothed me.

I let go of my concerns and took in the space around us. New York truly was the city that never slept. There were people everywhere——thankfully not in the dimly lit back alley. Still, they helped to camouflage us as we waited for the signal from Tony that he'd neutralized the guards. And while Adriano had wanted to shoot them from a nearby building, the Chicago guys had vetoed it, preferring to go in quietly.

Puffs of fog formed in front of us as our breath mixed with the cold air. The chill settled into my bones, and I shifted from foot to foot before Nico pulled me into his arms, my back to his chest, to share his heat. We'd worn insulated coats that were thin and flexible enough not to deter our movements. We'd strapped guns beneath the jackets in shoulder holsters and waistbands, shoving extra magazines into every available pocket. Emiliana had gifted me a cool spring-loaded arm sheath that would release the knife it held with a flick of my wrist. And I wanted to use it. Badly. She'd shown me her badass sleek, old-world Karambit knives that would carve some serious damage from our enemies.

Ricco and Joey were my targets. I wasn't picky. Either one would do.

I felt Nico stiffen, and my focus flew to the back door where Tony was headed, and a small group of men had just been admitted. When he reached the lone guard, he flicked his lit cigarette to the ground. A flash of silver glinted as he arced his hand back, connecting with the soldier's throat as Adriano shot out the camera. Tony caught the man before he fell. It was almost too easy, and I could tell by the way Nico waited another half a second that he'd thought the same thing.

Tony slung his arm around the man to support his weight while he bled out then half dragged him to a nearby dumpster. A group of our soldiers strolled by and covered Tony's actions as he shoved the almost-dead man behind it.

We were cleared to move. Nico and I were first. Everyone else would trickle in, going in different directions and taking multiple exit paths from the club with the victims, which we hoped would lessen the chances of an ambush of guards. They, too, would be forced to split up and weave through the crowds inside. A majority of our guards would remain outside, keeping the perimeter secure so that no one entered through the back or the side doors, which were too visible for our primary entry point.

Nico and I walked along the alleyway to the door. An over-head light shone in a semicircle around it, and we stopped under the dim glow. I punched the code into the panel on the left of the door to unlock it, praying they hadn't changed it from the last time I'd spied on the soldiers coming and going.

When the lock slid free, I breathed a sigh of relief then drew my gun, letting it lead the way beside Nico's. A slight scuff sounded behind me, but I didn't turn. It was the others. I led Nico down the same stairwell I'd raced through when I'd fled the building. Nico and Sofia would be taking the elevator and another hallway, as would the rest of the Chicago Mafia, Dante, and Cal. Adriano was stationed outside with his sniper rifle.

Our descent was silent, the sounds from the club muted as we hurried to the lower level. Nico took point at our entry, his hand easing the steel door open. Low murmurs of men filtered through, and I blocked out what I knew was happening.

I waited in the stairwell as the door clicked shut behind him. Even with the scuffle muffled, my heart rate increased. We'd known someone would be on guard there, and Nico had insisted on neutralizing them before I came through.

I leaned back on the railing and looked up, making sure no one else was coming. When the door opened and I saw it was Nico, I lowered my gun. After I eased through the entrance, he stuffed the body off to the side in the stairwell while I kept watch.

Then we were both in the hallway. There were cameras in the corners. Nico shot them as we went forward, blowing our cover—but it was necessary. I led the way to the wing we were in charge of liberating. We'd used Dante's blueprints to assign who would be where. Voices filtered down the hall, and Nico and I raced to intercept as two men rounded the corner.

One was short and burly, odd-looking next to his lean counterpart. Shock registered on their faces as they reached for their guns. My finger squeezed the trigger once for the heart then higher. A small hole formed in the center of the shorter man's forehead before he crumpled to the ground. Nico had disposed of the taller one.

We raced forward, only stopping to swipe keys from one of the guards. We could open the doors more quickly that way. We stepped over the corpses then rounded the corner to the wing where I'd been held. A few men were leaving rooms, and we quickly disposed of them. There were no windows on the steel doors. I took the right, struggling to find the correct keys to turn the locks, and he got to work on the left side.

The next fifteen minutes were straight out of a horror show as we found the women locked away in various states of abuse. Few had clothes. Most were bruised and bloody. Ten of the rooms were occupied, two of them with men inside too. The men's deaths were too quick for my liking, but we needed to get the women to safety.

Tears pricked my eyes as I slid my arm around a young woman who was barely conscious. The ones who were strong enough helped the others. Somehow, we made it back to the stairwell with our precious cargo in tow.

As we waited while Nico made a call, I glanced down another hallway to see Emiliana wielding curved and bloody blades, slicing her way through more of the depraved men and soldiers who were down her and Stefano's wing to clear.

"We need a pickup. Rear door." Nico's voice snapped me back to the present, and I slammed a wall on my emotions.

In the few minutes we had been inside, the alarm had been raised, and soldiers poured into the bowels of the club. But we were ready. Gunshots rang out, and my pulse kicked up a notch with the urgency to liberate everyone who needed our help.

With great effort, I strained my muscles to work harder and faster to get the women to safety. It took five times as long to climb the stairs in their weakened state, but we made it. Tony was waiting in the alley, and the back doors of an SUV opened. It was freezing, and most of the women didn't have clothes, but there was a stack of blankets waiting for them on one of the seats.

Nico and I helped them climb in while Tony stood guard. A shout rang out. I worked faster, practically shoving the woman I was helping to catch the brunette Nico had let go of as shots were fired. Three women were stuck in the building and paused at the opened door. Eyes wide, they looked to me as if begging me to tell them what to do. Nico had moved forward to engage.

I motioned for them to stay where they were then peeked through the car window as five guards, including Dom, barreled down on us. Adriano picked off one after another, but he wasn't in a position to cover the entire alleyway. A small section that would be blind, which he'd warned us about when we'd gone over the blueprints. Dom dashed forward.

More shouts drew my focus to the building. Three men burst from the stairwell, guns aimed at the women hovering by the door. One rushed forward. Bullets peppered the ground. She stumbled as the other two ducked then collapsed inches from me. In rapid succession, I squeezed the trigger, hitting two men, but one advanced.

Glass shattered. I had to bend down, using the steel door as cover. Fractured shards rained on my head. Our guards swarmed seconds after the first shot was fired, but the damage had been done. The girl who had dashed forward was lying dead at my feet. The other two were coated in splatters of blood that I hoped wasn't theirs. Someone put down the last guard before he could do any more damage. All three lay in heaps inside. I stepped forward, free from the door to block for the girls. "Run!"

They hesitated, and Dom advanced, dropping one of the men he'd used as a human shield to fire repeatedly at Nico and Tony.

"No!" I couldn't help the scream that tore through my throat as one of Dom's bullets found its intended target. My mind played tricks on me, and I couldn't tell which one of our guys had fallen.

Uncaring of what I raced into, I darted forward, forgetting the women. The light that had hindered my sight where they'd fought cleared. And when I dropped to my knees, it was to the sight of Tony on the ground with Nico applying pressure to a stomach wound with one hand as he extended the other, firing at Dom.

All I could think of as I raised my gaze from Tony to Nico was that I could have lost him. Reality crashed back with a vengeance as I realized I still could. Dom barreled down on us, aiming his Glock. I didn't think before acting as I launched myself at Nico.

CHAPTER TWENTY

NICO

Mia screamed, her body slamming into me as a bullet whizzed by, burning a trail against my ear. Sheer terror sliced through me, and I gripped her tightly as I returned fire. When a satisfying hole appeared in a mammoth guard's forehead, I shifted my focus to her as our men took over securing the area. I raised my hands to grip either side of her face, inspecting for wounds. I couldn't get my heart to slow at the horror of what had happened, how she'd used her body as a shield.

"Baby, fuck." *Please be okay.* "Trey!" I bellowed, never taking my eyes from her beautiful face. She blinked, her mouth forming words that I couldn't hear in the panic over her well-being roaring in my ears.

Tony moaned on the ground in front of us. A human shield of guards surrounded us as shouting came from every direction. Mia's words pierced through the static in my mind, bringing reality on their heels.

"I'm okay." Her hands cupped my face, mirroring mine.

I shifted us out of the way as Trey pushed through the men

only to drop to his knees and bark orders for what he needed. They needed me, but I had to make sure Mia wasn't hurt. "What were you thinking?" I couldn't deal with what she'd done.

"Dom was going to shoot you in the head." Panic drained the color from her cheeks that had begun to return. "I had to." She shook her head frantically. "I couldn't live with myself if something happened to you."

I crushed her to me, holding her tightly as my heart continued to race, the truth of her act sinking in. She had been willing to sacrifice her life for mine. Any fraction of doubt I'd held on to regarding her intentions went up in flames.

My heart opened fully to her. "Mia—"

"Nico!" Trey shouted, and I released her before dropping to my knees on the other side of Tony's body, unable to continue our conversation. "I need your help."

Mia scrambled back, giving us space. Sirens whirled in the distance, and pedestrians screamed and ran. At the opening to the alley, people flooded out the front entrance of the club once word traveled about the shoot-out, pouring into the streets and adding chaos to an already out-of-control situation. We had minutes, if that, before law enforcement would arrive.

I pushed everything aside and focused on what needed to be done. I couldn't believe I'd forgotten that Tony had been shot. Blood saturated his clothes from the stomach wound he'd sustained. Trey issued instructions, and I placed my hand where he told me to while he set up a field IV that Tom, captain of my family's guard, held from where he stood by Tony's head.

Trey pushed the contents of a syringe into the IV as Tony convulsed, his skin taking on a sickly gray pallor. As the medicine worked its way into Tony's bloodstream, he sank into unconsciousness that I hoped was blissful.

Around us, the chaos slowly dissipated so that only a few were present in the back alley as Trey worked on Tony with practiced fervor. Trey maintained his focus, removing the bullet and doing what he could to stabilize Tony so we could move him.

The pavement was slick with blood, and bodies from the shoot-out lay scattered both inside and out. Our men had flooded the building, clearing out Tucci soldiers before returning to our vehicles or standing by for additional coverage while we worked.

Reports from the others sounded through our earpieces as the teams made it back to the hotel. The rescued women were being cared for. The only one badly injured on our team was Tony. I took one look at Tom's grim face and dreaded the conversation he would have with Nicole, Tony's mother and the woman Tom had been seriously courting. I asked the question that I knew burned in Tom's mind. "Will he make it?"

"It's too soon to tell." Trey had deposited the bullet he'd removed onto a blue rectangle that held his instruments. He did what he could to staunch the flow of blood before transport, issuing orders about what medical equipment he would need.

It was the worst possible scenario. I wished it had happened in Chicago, where Trey had a room set up in his home with every piece of equipment and instrument he could possibly need. But in New York, we were scrambling.

Adriano stepped forward on Tom's right. "I'll have it arranged. Bring him to our house. Whatever you need will be there when we arrive."

No one asked any questions. Tony's life hung in the balance, and we had to trust Adriano. Several of us carefully lifted Tony while Trey kept pressure on the wound. Another van waited nearby, and Tom grabbed a clean blanket from the stash reserved for the victims we'd rescued.

After Tony was secure and the van pulled away from the curb with care, I took my first full breath. Tom had gone in the van with Trey and Tony, and I watched through the window as he lifted his phone to his ear, remorse clear in his expression.

I scanned the surrounding area, searching for Mia. When one of the guards walked by, I grabbed him by the arm. "Have you seen Mia?"

"No."

I released him before he could speak again and barked the question into our comm device. A series of no's came back, and a whoosh of panic set in as I realized I'd missed something in the chaos.

Mia

I stood helplessly while Nico assisted Trey in saving Tony's life. With each demand to bring more blankets, tools, or a van, I was shuffled farther away from the action. My stomach rolled as I took in how much blood had soaked Tony's clothes.

A little away from the circle of men helping to save a life, I glanced around, making sure we hadn't missed anything. Something still felt off, but it could have been because there had been no reports of Ricco on the premises. It wasn't unheard of, but for some reason, I was sure he would be there.

When a wave of fatigue rolled over me as the rush of adrenaline faded, I moved to lean against the building, careful to stay out of their way but not straying too far. A van pulled to the curb. One of the Chicago soldiers jumped out of the passenger seat and rounded to the back, flinging open the doors. Another man barreled past me with a mattress tucked under his arm then flung it into the back of the van. Someone spread a blanket on it, and I watched as Trey and Tom carefully lifted Tony and slid him into the van.

I felt rather than heard a presence at my back and went to turn but was stopped when a hand holding a cloyingly sweet rag clapped over my mouth. A wave of dizziness overcame me, and my knees buckled. I knew I'd made a grave mistake by distancing myself from the safety of my newfound family.

CHAPTER TWENTY-ONE

MIA

Disoriented, I slowly inhaled, deciphering why I felt so horrible. With a rush of adrenaline, it came to me. My shitty stepbrother had drugged me again. I couldn't believe it. It wasn't the first time I'd fallen prey to that. Anger burned through me, helping to chase the cobwebs away but not the dull chloroform headache. What I found most interesting though was the lack of restraints. I cracked open my eyelids, gradually letting the light in.

It was quiet, aside from the faint rhythmic sound of waves. *Am I at the Jersey Shore?* That was the only fathomable explanation as I remembered that Ricco's family had once owned a home here, unless he had flown us somewhere. But I couldn't get behind that thought. He craved power, and to remove himself from his Mafia dream of becoming boss seemed farfetched.

I guessed it was early in the morning, given how the light cut through the partially opened blinds. There were bars on the window. *Is that a new addition or something that was original to the house?* Either way, it effectively shut down any thought to escape through there.

The room was sparse—a dresser, bed, lamp, and two doors. My guess was that one was for the closet, the other for the exit. That was the one I wanted. I ran my hands down my thighs, delighted that I was still wearing the same clothes I'd had on the night before. My guns were missing, but I found the choke wire and several small knives intact when I checked the hidden pockets. A slow grin spread across my lips in anticipation of surprising Ricco with them.

Pots banged, and my stomach growled. I didn't care. What got my attention was the slight scent of brewed coffee coming from somewhere in the house. If Ricco didn't bring me a cup, I would kill him on principle.

The walls were thin, and I could hear sounds clearly from what I could only guess was the kitchen. Needing to stretch my legs and hopefully break out of there, I curled my toes, testing for numbness. I found none, so I pushed to a sitting position and slid my legs over the bed to the wood floor. It was cold, and I shivered from the chill.

As I stood, the door opened. My asshole stepbrother filled the opening with his bulky body, a steaming mug of coffee in his hand. I decided his execution could wait a few minutes.

"I brought you coffee."

I crossed my arms over my chest, my need to harm him warring with wariness. "I'm not stupid enough to drink anything you give me."

He rolled his eyes and took a sip before extending his arm to pass it to me. "There. Not poisoned."

I snorted. "It is now." But I was too desperate for the caffeine hit to turn it down. I made sure to position my lips on the opposite side of the mug then took a satisfying gulp.

It was rich and strong, with only a hint of creamer, exactly how I liked my first cup. The second could be sweeter, but that first hit needed to kick-start my morning with a jolt. "Why am I here? I'm already married, so your evil plot won't work."

He leaned against the doorjamb, crossing his legs at the ankles in a very relaxed pose that made me hyperaware of whatever he would say. Everything he did was for a reason. And to lull me into a sense of security with the lack of bindings, the coffee, and his relaxed body language... It couldn't be good.

"I brought you here so we could have a little chat. There are many things Joey has kept from you."

He got me there. I was going to bite, even though it wasn't in my best interest. "Like what?" Another fortifying sip of coffee. Maybe a little more. I downed all but a quarter of it, needing the powerful punch it packed.

His deep chuckle filled the room. "In time. For now, come join me for breakfast."

My stomach cheered him on while the rest of me couldn't decide if I should attack him now or after eating. So I followed him, well aware that it wouldn't end well for me.

Since I had the time, I thought I would fish for a little information. "Nice touch with the bomb at one of the Chicago-owned clubs."

Ricco chuckled. "That was Guido's doing." He met my gaze with cold, dead eyes. "You underestimate him too often."

Warning received.

It wasn't until we were in the small eat-in kitchen area that I saw what he had in store for me—Guido sat casually at the table with his cup of coffee. The former Amato underboss probably still thought that marrying me could help him win back his position in the family.

"What's he doing here?" I stopped before I got too close. They were both snakes. I had no idea what they would do next.

"Don't be rude, sister dear."

I made a gagging sound. "So sorry, I just threw up in my mouth." *"Sister." Please.*

Guido curled his lip, clearly disgusted. Good. I wanted him

to stay far away from me. I glanced around the space. It was homey but small. "Where am I?"

"This was where Mom and I lived before Joey killed my father. A little slice of the past."

"Hmm, and you come back here often? How sentimental of you." I plucked a blueberry muffin from the table. "You had time for a bakery run?"

Ricco shrugged. "You were out cold, and it's not like Nico will find you here. The house is registered in Mom's maiden name."

Don't be too sure. I broke off a piece of the sweet-smelling pastry, plopped it in my mouth, and chewed slowly. "What's the plan? I'm free to go after this heartwarming breakfast?"

A crash sounded as Guido slammed his fist on the table. Silverware rattled from the vibration of his temper tantrum. "You will not be leaving unless it's with me."

"Yeah, that'll be a hard pass." I itched to bury one of my hidden blades in Guido's smug face.

"You won't have much choice in the matter, Mia." Ricco's hard, beady eyes held a hint of excitement. *Shit.* I was well versed in that expression and knew what would happen next. I dropped the muffin to the table and moved for one of the knives hidden in a seam of my pants.

Ricco lunged for me with his hands outstretched and his face contorted with hatred. I dodged him, sinking my short blade just above his heart. His hands clawed my shoulders, preventing me from putting any space between us. Pulling my knife out, I jabbed at him again in his soft middle. His rough hands moved to my neck, squeezing. I couldn't draw a breath. Black spots freckled my vision, and dizziness made my knees weak.

He swatted the weapon from my hand, only needing one to grip my neck. The black dots swimming in my vision increased until I succumbed and passed out.

There was nothing gradual about my return to consciousness. I gasped as I came to with a jolt. Adrenaline coursed through my body, my heart pounding a fist-thumping beat. Loud laughter echoed through the small space, and I could only assume that was what had awakened me.

As quickly as I could, I cataloged my situation. Something loose and soft covered my legs, and I glanced down. That fucker. Ricco had stripped off my pants, probably in front of the perv Guido, and replaced them with gray sweats rolled at the waist and ankles.

Since there wasn't anything I could do about it, I glanced around at the parts of the room I could see. The bay window with its gaudy curtains and a loud white couch with blue flowers were to my left, which meant the kitchen table was to my right. A tarp was beneath me, barely cushioning my stretched-out position on the wood floor. This time, I didn't have the luxury of waking without restraints.

My arms were tied and secured over my head. I couldn't move them or my legs—they were tethered to something to keep them straight along the floor. A large jug of water thumped next to my head. Ricco appeared in my line of sight right before he placed a wet washcloth over my nose and mouth.

Ricco dropped to a knee and grabbed my chin in a tight grip. I shot daggers at him with my eyes, struggling as much as I could against the bindings. Guido appeared on my other side, leaning over me with that stupid, malicious smile he wore far too often. I wanted to smack it off his ugly mug.

"You need to be taught a lesson," Guido murmured as he scanned my body from head to foot.

Gross. *When I get out of this predicament, I will happily gouge his eyes out.*

"This fun little exercise in obedience was Guido's idea." Ricco smirked, holding my chin tightly. "He preferred I didn't leave marks. He wanted something to look forward to with you tonight when he takes you back to his place."

I shrieked in outrage, but my voice was cut short as Ricco slapped a wet cloth over my face then poured water over it, flooding my mouth. I did my best to close my throat, but it was no use. I was helpless as water invaded my screaming lungs, my body convinced I was drowning.

When he stopped the downpour and twisted me to my side with a brutal hit to my back, I spewed water, gasped, and struggled to drag air in. He repeated the process several more times, and with each one, I went through the same motions, drowning then vomiting water and gasping for air when he relented and turned me onto my side.

I shivered from the cold water that soaked my face, hair, and chest. Shock and panic gripped me as tightly as the restraints.

Ricco played my body like a puppet but not my mind. That was still my own. A deep-rooted anger and a need for revenge pushed aside the building panic. I would make both of them pay.

Flipped to my side, the wet cloth removed, I hacked and spewed water. Sucking in air as he turned me to my back, I struggled against his hold and the rope, desperate to get free. "I will fucking kill you!"

Ricco chuckled. "Yeah, you're a real threat right now."

He slapped the cloth back over my face and upended the water jug. My body thrashed as much as I could against the bindings, blind panic taking over me as water replaced the air in my lungs.

Over and over, he toyed with me until much later, when he grew tired of drowning me. He removed the wet cloth and sat back on his heels, studying me like a bug he'd just tortured under a magnifying glass. When I was able to talk instead of cough, I growled in a stuttered vow my disgust over his stupid plan. "Guido can't have me."

"That's where you're wrong." I sensed Ricco's renewed interest. The waterboarding had gotten old, but the conversation seemed to entertain him. "Guido has been permitted to take you home."

What fresh bullshit is this? "By whom?" My voice grew stronger the less I coughed and wheezed. "Guido has no right. And you have no authority in the family business. In fact, I'm not even family anymore."

Ricco's laugh was filled with evil intent, and chills erupted over my body. "Oh, Mia. Guido is the least of your worries. Your father is coming, and he's not happy about the raid on his business or your betrayal."

CHAPTER TWENTY-TWO

NICO

The sun was coming up, and I was no closer to finding Mia. My jaw ached from clenching my teeth. *How was it possible that she was there one minute, and not a single person had seen her leave?*

Ricco was the only one spotted in the club. Joey and Guido were nowhere on the premises. Somehow, Ricco had taken her. And this time, he would die.

Throughout the remainder of the night, Enzo and Adriano had searched through a camera feed they were able to access online with the help of Hailey, Trey's wife, who was back in Chicago. She had managed to find a brief snapshot of Ricco with Mia, who was unconscious. But that was the extent of it. With all the chaos, they'd been lost in a sea of panicking clubgoers, Torrid's staff, and pedestrians.

Stefano had tracked down Joey and demanded Mia's return, but her father swore he knew nothing of her abduction. And in turn, he'd called for the return of what had been stolen from him after Mia had fled, which made little sense to us—but Dante had stiffened. He'd played a role, for sure, but that wasn't our concern.

Sofia had done what she could to keep me calm until exhaustion claimed her. It had helped, at least outwardly. I was a bundle of nerves and rage inside. I couldn't help but think of worst-case scenarios. The only thing that kept me sane was that Ricco, Guido, and Joey all wanted to use her, so they would keep her alive.

It was tense in the Verretti household. We were in a Manhattan building owned by Dante's family. Tony was in surgery in one of the rooms. The longer it took, the more anxious everyone became. I glanced at Tom, who often got Sofia duty when she was younger and who all the women in the families swore resembled an older and much larger Jensen Ackles. He spoke in hushed tones on the phone to Nicole, Tony's mom.

My sister was curled up in Enzo's lap, sound asleep. Emiliana and Stefano had their heads bent together, whispering. Marco and El had volunteered to comb the streets and requestion the guards in search of a clue about Mia's whereabouts.

That left the Verretti brothers. I sank into a chair at the dining room table, where Adriano stared at his computer screen. Cal leaned over his shoulder, and Dante hadn't taken his eyes off me the entire time.

"You care about her." Dante's deep voice boomed through the hushed group.

I pivoted to glare at him. "She's my wife." I had nothing to prove.

Unfazed, he leaned back in his chair and continued to regard me. "I've known Mia her entire life. We all have." He nodded toward his brothers. "We care about her and will find her."

I leaned down, my palms flat on the table between us. "If you care about her so much, why did you let Ricco terrorize her when she was younger? And how about how her father locked her in the house for most of her life?"

"You're aware of how some of the others in the Chicago

Mafia were treated by their fathers. Maybe not then, but you are now. Did you help them?"

He meant Stefano and Lil. It was a fair point, but I wasn't in the mood to agree. "You were given an opportunity to help her. You turned it down, which I'm glad you did. It brought her into my life. But because of that, I don't believe that you have her best interests at heart."

"There are circumstances"—he shared a look with his brothers—"we're still unsure of. The evening Mia and I had planned to raid the trucks was when I would get her away from the Tucci household."

I called bullshit. "And how would you do that? She answered to her father at that point, not you. By taking her, the Verrettis would have declared war on her family."

A muscle jumped along the side of Dante's jaw, the only visible sign that I'd hit a nerve. "It's something we should have done years ago. But it wasn't until recently that we learned more about her situation."

Closed doors could hide a lot. Lil had shared her experiences with my sister, and Emiliana had learned as much about Stefano. I opened my mouth to question what he'd learned when Trey appeared.

Exhaustion painted deep half-circles beneath his eyes as he grabbed a tumbler half full of whiskey out of Stefano's hand and slammed it back. None of us said a word, preferring to give him a moment before he told us Tony's prognosis.

Trey dropped to a chair and rubbed a hand over his face before he raised his eyes to meet ours. "He made it."

Half the fight drained from me at his words. Tony had been a difficult man to like for a long time, but after Max returned, everything changed. Then Antonio Caruso was killed, freeing his wife, Nicole, and son from his iron-fisted control. Tony became one of us, whereas before, we'd tolerated him only because we had to.

"When can he go home?" Stefano stood, pulling Em to her feet.

"I want to give him a few hours," Trey said. "He's stable, but it would be better to wait to move him."

Sofia blinked sleepy eyes at our brother before sliding off Enzo's lap. "Enz and I'll sit with Tony so you can get some sleep."

"We'll wake you if there's any change." Enzo clasped Sofia's hand as they left to sit with Tony.

"We can leave late afternoon," Trey said to Stefano before turning to Dante. "Where can I crash?"

"I'll show you to a room." Cal unfurled himself to his over-six-foot height before leading the way to the hallway, where there were several bedrooms.

I glanced at Stefano. "Any news from Marco?"

"No." Stefano looked as angry as I felt. "He and El are on their way back."

"I've got something," Adriano interrupted, his gaze glued to the laptop's screen.

"Where is she?" All family dynamics evaporated as I demanded answers. I didn't care about anything but finding Mia.

"I'm not positive, but it's the best shot we've got." Adriano's mercurial eyes bore into me. "Ricco lived near the Jersey Shore with his parents before he moved into the Tucci household with his mom." He turned the screen so that I could see an image from Google Maps of a modern stucco one-story home on the shore.

I memorized the address then headed toward the door.

"Hold on, Nico." Stefano grabbed my arm, but I yanked it free. "We're going with you." When Dante and Adriano stood, Stefano shook his head. "It's better with only Nico, Em, and me. You need to stay in case Trey needs anything else for Tony."

We raced to the underground parking, where we'd left the

cars. I had to drive. If I didn't, I would go crazy with worry. When the elevator doors opened with a quiet whoosh, we rushed into the garage and to the closest car.

Stefano tossed me a set of keys before opening the back door for Em. She slid across the seat and gave my shoulder a reassuring squeeze as Stefano settled into the passenger seat. He barely had his door closed before I slammed my foot on the accelerator and tore out of the garage, my only concern that I make it there while she was still alive.

CHAPTER TWENTY-THREE

MIA

After Ricco informed me that my father was en route and had approved my marriage to Guido, he went back to waterboarding—"for fun." His words. As for me, I would enjoy shooting him, also "for fun."

Guido had gone out to pick up lunch and was due back soon. He'd had his fill of watching me suffer at my sadistic stepbrother's hands. Dark intent had etched itself in the sadistic curve of his thin lips.

Ricco leaned back on his heels, finally removing the washcloth from my face and watching me struggle to take a full breath without coughing. There were worse tortures to withstand, but it wasn't a walk in the park.

"Are you done with me?" I wanted to know when Joey would be there and whether he'd sanctioned the playtime session for his favorite adopted son. Ricco's reaction told me what I hadn't asked. The slow smile and unhurried way he stood was enough to know that Joey was livid. A wave of fear wormed its way into my psyche. I knew what he was capable of, and I worried that being his daughter wasn't enough to still his hand.

"For now." He left my line of sight, and seconds later, the

rope holding my arms went slack. I jerked them over my head and down to my waist, leaning to the side so I could push myself into a sitting position.

Ricco grabbed my wrists and dragged me closer. There was a flash of a blade, and my heart skipped a beat. The rope tightened, biting into my flesh, then I was free as the severed ends fell away. He bent and did the same to my ankles. I scrambled back before gaining my feet.

I eyed the door, but there was no way I could get past him. Instead, I scanned the area, looking for weapons. I made a silent note to get my deadly pants back before I left that hellhole, preferably with Ricco in a pool of blood and long gone from this lifetime.

"We should talk before Dad gets here and Guido returns with lunch." Ricco leaned against the island, his arms crossed over his chest.

Not good. I didn't like the way he spoke or how he was eyeing me. I was prey. Nothing new, but it unsettled me more than it used to because of how differently Nico and his family treated me.

"What?" I mirrored his posture.

"You need to go with Guido. It's the best move for you. If you stay…" He shrugged, lowered his chin, then ran his tongue over his teeth while holding my gaze. A flash of cruelty darkened his eyes, and I had to fight the shiver that threatened to give away how he affected me.

"Can't do that." I raised my chin, defying him. "I'm married to Nico. The capo bore witness, and Dad has a signed copy of the marriage license."

"Doesn't matter. He'll get it annulled. And we don't answer to Stefano."

My mouth fell open, and I had to work to close it. *Wow.* "You do realize he is the boss of *all* bosses."

"Not in New York."

"You're an idiot."

"And you're nothing but a bargaining chip. Have a nice life as Guido's bitch."

I was no one's pawn. I'd proven that when I left and forged my own destiny. I launched myself at him, beyond disgusted. My fist slammed into his face, and he laughed. Pain exploded along my cheek from his return strike, and my head whipped to the side, my body helpless but to follow the trajectory of the punch. My hip hit the hideous couch, and I half fell onto it and the floor before recovering.

I got to my feet to go after him again, despite what he had done to me, when the door slammed against the wall. My father stood framed in the opening, red infusing his cheeks, his eyes narrowed to slits. His right hand was bandaged from where he'd been shot, and a trill of satisfaction went through me upon seeing it.

"Sit down!" he boomed.

My legs buckled, and I fell onto the couch then scowled. Years of ingrained habits were hard to break. But break them, I would. I already had—I'd left. I had to keep reminding myself so he wouldn't get the best of me.

"Why are you here?" I asked, wanting him to get whatever he had to say to me over with. Just being in his presence made me want to vomit.

The door closed behind him, the audible click of the lock loud in the pregnant silence. I held my tongue, refusing to say another word, waiting him out. I couldn't understand why he wanted to speak to me. He'd made his disdain clear in our last meeting. And there was no way the marriage would be annulled, so I couldn't understand what he hoped to gain.

Ricco remained by the island as my father strolled toward me as if there on a Sunday visit. He stopped in front of me then moved almost as quickly as Ricco had. Pain exploded a second time across my cheek from his backhanded strike.

I righted myself, swallowing the whimper that begged for voice. There was no way I would give him the satisfaction. Still, I said nothing more.

"Get up." He barked his order, and I obeyed, unwilling to take another hit to the same spot.

We stood before one another, my back to the window and his to Ricco. Foolish move on his part, as if he didn't know that Ricco would stab him in the back if the slightest chance of taking over the family without repercussions presented itself. I had no doubt that was already in the works. Guido had a similar goal, only that idiot had been found out, stripped of his title of underboss, and banished from the Amato family. Ricco, however, was much more cunning, and I had no doubt that he would accomplish his goal... if I didn't kill him first. That was very much on the table.

"What I have to say to you will be the last time we'll speak." My father drew himself to his full height and looked down his nose as he delivered his speech. "You want to know about your mother and what happened?"

I couldn't help it. I was desperate for any little detail about the woman I'd lost when I was young. "Yes."

"She was the most beautiful woman I'd ever seen. I met her not long after I'd taken over as boss for the family. I hadn't planned to take a wife so early. I wanted to wait, but I couldn't get her out of my mind. She consumed my thoughts to the point of distraction. So I married her and gave her everything she ever could have wanted."

Really? Knowing him, I found that hard to believe. "Even the freedom to come and go? To do things that she wanted?"

His upper lip curled into a sneer. "You're an ungrateful child. I should have beaten you more often to curb that unflattering stubborn streak you have. It's from her, you know."

"Good." Satisfaction swelled despite the pain I knew would follow. And it did, in the form of another backhand to the same fucking spot on my face. I barely refrained from touching my lip. Warmth trickled down my chin from the split lip that was swelling badly. "I see you wanted me to look my best for what's coming? Would that be polygamy? Because you know I'm already married in the eyes of the church, God, and the capo—who's *your boss.*"

There was a knock at the door, and once Joey gave a slight nod, Ricco opened it, letting Guido in with several brown bags that smelled like greasy fast food. My father notched his head toward the table, and Guido took a seat. I could tell he wanted to dig in, but that would have been foolish before my father gave him the go-ahead. He didn't have any grounds to stand on, and we all knew he was lucky to be there.

"I change my mind, daughter. I was going to allow you to marry Guido. I thought it was the least I could do, considering he would be taking over the Amato family. And to keep the alliances in New York where they should be. But your insolence is too great."

Guido began to protest but wisely shut his trap when Joey held up a hand.

"Let's continue with the story, shall we?" His brows rose, and I kept my mouth shut. "Your mother should have been happy. I gave her everything her heart could desire. But she was young and foolish. She betrayed me and had an affair with Arturo Verretti."

Dante's father? Holy shit. I couldn't help but wonder if Dante knew about it.

"Of course, I found out. It was the ultimate betrayal. So I did what I had to, despite how she'd broken my heart."

You don't have a heart. I pressed my lips together so I didn't spew my thoughts.

"I ordered my captain to shoot her. And"—he moved toward the door, opening it to leave as he cast a heated glance at Ricco, who straightened—"you know the rest of the story, which brings us to your fate. You, too, have betrayed me, and you will suffer a similar fate. As history repeats itself, it's fitting that the captain's son should carry out my order to kill you."

Nico

I cursed the traffic as we pulled off the highway and onto the exit that would take us to the address where Ricco had lived with his parents when he was young. It'd been about fourteen years since he had resided there. Adriano Verretti had shown us that the house had been registered in his mother's name, and I couldn't believe we'd missed it until almost two hours ago.

The closer we came, the more I drove like an asshole, weaving around cars and speeding along the shoulder. But every minute counted. I'd told Sof to make sure our brother stayed until he got word from me. I would have preferred he was along for the ride, but Tony needed Trey there. I only hoped that we wouldn't too.

I was blind to the scenery, only concerned with the next turn and the one after that. My nerves were shot. Stefano and Em understood and maintained their silence. It wasn't much farther.

Not even ten minutes later, the white stucco house came into view. Two cars were in the driveway, and I eased my foot off the accelerator, pulling to the curb a few houses down so they wouldn't spot us. We needed the element of surprise.

We got out, not bothering to close the doors. We flew to the closest window on silent feet, our guns leading the way. Without discussing it, we split up. Em took the side, Stefano had the front door, and I went around back.

Loud voices volleyed back and forth, increasing in volume the closer I got to the screen door. Hunched down, I neared a window that didn't have any blinds to block my view. It was the one above the sink. Mia was at the other end of the room, her back to the bay windows.

Everything in me froze. Ricco stood before her, pointing a gun at her chest. But he was looking at Guido, who stood near the back door, gesturing wildly with his arms. I didn't have time to figure out what was going on. Ricco could squeeze the trigger at any moment, and then I would be too late.

I rushed forward, ripped the screen door open, slammed my shoulder into the back door, and launched myself at Ricco. I gripped his wrist, squeezing as I wrenched the barrel down and away from Mia. A bullet discharged, and my worst nightmare came true.

Mia jerked back then stumbled to the floor right as I landed on top of Ricco, a sickening crack sounding when his head hit the wood. The gun clattered across the floor, and Mia lunged forward as I realized mine had also fallen when I'd tackled him.

Another shot went off as my fingers curled around the handle of my knife. Ricco bucked, twisting, and we rolled. Footsteps echoed as Stefano and Em rushed into the chaos.

"You're too late," Ricco growled as he fought to gain the upper hand. "She's already marked for death."

A red haze filtered my vision, and I brought the knife up and across his neck in one smooth swipe. Blood pulsed from the severed arteries. I pushed back onto my heels as Ricco's hands flew to his neck to staunch the blood flow. It was no use, and the room filled with his desperate gurgles until there were no more.

Then I was up and on my feet, scrambling to where Mia lay, her arm outstretched and fingers encircling Ricco's Glock. I glanced at where it was pointed to find Guido bleeding from a chest wound, not even two feet from her.

I pulled her into my arms and put pressure over the bullet wound in her leg. Blood soaked into her wet pants, and she shivered in my arms. Despite how pale she was, the split lip, and swelling on one side of her face, her smile was brilliant. I wanted to kill him all over again.

"I knew you would come," Mia said before her eyes closed, and she went limp in my arms.

CHAPTER TWENTY-FOUR

NICO

"She's lost too much blood." I glared at Stefano in the rearview mirror as he drove us back to the Verretti residence with Em in the passenger seat and Mia curled on my lap in the back. She'd lost too much blood, and I'd had to apply a tourniquet. "Go to a hospital."

"It's not critical." His voice was calm. Too calm.

All it did was fuel my anger, and I tensed. "I don't care."

"It's not what we do, and you know that." He flicked his gaze to mine in the mirror before returning it to the road in front of him, increasing speed until we were flying down the highway.

I couldn't get the image of Mia bleeding on the floor out of my head. With the pad of my fingers, I smoothed her hair from her face and held her close. I wanted to fight with Stefano and make him turn the car around and head to the nearest hospital.

"It's a gunshot wound," Em said. "You know we can't do that. Besides, Trey is the best."

Em was right, even if it killed me that it would take time to get to him.

The rational part of my brain knew she would be fine, but I

was discovering I couldn't be rational when it came to Mia. The drive to Trey was the longest two hours of my life.

When we pulled into the underground parking lot, I lifted her from the car and carried her to the elevator in long strides. A Verretti guard was waiting for us and gave us access to the floor where Trey would be.

Mia had awoken twice in the car but then passed out again. A bruise on her temple and a fist-sized one on her cheek made me want to kill Ricco all over again. Fury at Joey boiled beneath the surface, but we would deal with him.

As soon as the doors opened on the top floor, I bellowed for Trey. Mia's eyes flew open, her fingers fisting my blood-soaked shirt. She looked at it and then at me, horror filling her eyes. I shook my head. "It's not mine." Most was hers, the rest Ricco's, but I didn't want to frighten her more.

Dante and Cal came forward, but I clutched her tighter. There was no way I would relinquish her to anyone but Trey. I couldn't shake the rage from seeing Ricco's gun pointed at her.

When Trey appeared, I followed him to where Tony was in post-op recovery. He was still unconscious. I shot Trey a questioning glance.

"He's doing well." Trey motioned to the second bed someone had set up after we'd called in Mia's condition while driving. "Put her there."

I lay her down and then threaded my fingers with hers. Her eyes were open, but she looked like she could pass out again at any second. I relayed everything that had happened while he cut the leg of her pants away then draped a clean sheet over part of her exposed skin before he slowly released the tourniquet in small increments and cleaned the wound. With each swipe of the gauze, blood welled.

"I have to get an IV started. Put pressure here," Trey instructed.

I did as he said. Once the IV was feeding fluids and medicine into her veins, I felt the edge of fear ebb. She would be fine, or so I was trying to convince myself. Too many things could go wrong.

As far as I could tell, nothing vital had been hit. The wound was to the muscle of her thigh. It could have been much worse.

"Nico." Sofia clutched my arm. "You need to go to the other room and tell them everything. I've got her."

"No." We all had gunshot and wound-care training—it was a necessity in our world. I'd already assessed her after she was shot. No arteries had been hit, but that didn't guarantee there wasn't more damage. I didn't want to leave her.

"Nic, you have to go talk to Marco and Dante. It's important. Go. I'll help Trey," Sofia insisted.

"It'll be easier with Sof," Trey murmured as he physically moved my hand away from Mia's wound.

"Stefano was there. He can fill them in."

"He wants you to because he wasn't there for all of it." Sofia's voice was patient but firm. "You'll be back in no time. Just handle that part."

I hated it, but they were right. Sofia could distance herself and work efficiently by Trey's side. Gritting my teeth, I stepped back and let my sister take over for me. But I would be back after talking with Marco and Dante. And why the hell did Dante need information? I still had my suspicions where he was concerned, despite how accommodating they'd been to the families taking over their house and territory.

Everyone was gathered in the living room: Stefano, Emiliana, Marco, El, Enzo, Dante, Cal, and Adriano. Even Tom, Marco's captain, was present. I kept tabs on Dante while going to the dry bar, where decanters of whiskey sat. Pouring two fingers, I downed it.

I relished the heat spreading through me from the whiskey as I struggled to compartmentalize my fear for Mia. I needed to focus on analyzing and strategizing.

Shifting my focus to Dante, that same swirl of mistrust gathered, and I narrowed my gaze at him. My fingers curled, itching for a computer to dive deeply into his life, searching for anything he was hiding. Something kept me from accepting the Verretti brothers' good intentions toward the Five Families. I didn't have an opinion about Cal yet. I was most comfortable with Adriano. He reminded me of Enzo but without as much humor.

I leaned against the bar and spoke to my brother. "I killed Ricco, and Guido is also dead."

"And Joey?" Marco asked.

"We didn't see him, and there wasn't anyone else in the house." I couldn't help but wonder what we would've found if we'd arrived sooner. "From the few seconds, I heard Ricco and Guido's argument. Joey had agreed to give Mia to him. It seems Joey changed his mind at the last minute and decided Ricco should kill her. We got there just in time."

"While you were gone, we came to an agreement with Dante and just cleared it with Stefano." A small tic formed in Marco's jaw where the muscle jumped. It was the only tell he had when something concerned him.

"What the hell is going on?" My gut churned with trepidation. Whatever they'd discussed was going to be something I would disagree with.

"The Tucci family took a devastating hit," Marco said. "By the time we left, the FBI was crawling all over the warzone we left them. Most of Ricco's soldiers were killed or seriously injured and apprehended."

"Why is this a problem?" There was something I was missing, and my gaze jumped back to Dante's. There was worry beneath the steely confidence he wore like a second skin. My instinct about him flared to life.

"Joey's working to put out fires," Dante said. "Cal leaked a video clip to the feds of Ricco and his men unloading abducted women into the building. The trafficking outfit has been shut down. Adriano is siphoning his bank accounts. The money stripped from profits on the women will be used to return them to health and their families or give them new lives elsewhere." As Dante explained what they were doing, Cal slipped from the room.

"Where are the victims?" While Mia was missing, I'd let the fallout sit heavily on Marco and Stefano's shoulders. It was time I reengaged. Mia was in good hands with my brother, the trauma surgeon.

"We have a large house in Long Island that'll work temporarily. Cal is working on purchasing a building and setting up contractors to have it converted to meet their needs with counselors, private rooms, recreation, and dining."

"And who will monitor you, Dante?" I wanted to know what was stopping him from taking over Joey's operation as his own.

"I was hoping Mia could be involved in running some of the programs or overseeing whatever she wanted to." Dante ignored the dig.

"Why?"

"Because it's her family who hurt them. It'll give her a sense of closure to be involved in helping the victims." Dante's tone never wavered.

I couldn't argue against that. It was a good idea and one I would discuss with her. "The decision will be hers." I dismissed Dante and addressed Marco. "What else?" I knew there was more.

"A commission has been called." Stefano stood after that statement.

Cal walked back in and gave a pointed look to Dante as he stood then left the way his brother had come. That was why I didn't trust him. The conversation directly affected him and his brothers, but he was leaving to do something else.

I narrowed my eyes at Marco, whose mouth was set in a

grim line, and couldn't help but wonder if that had to do with what Joey had claimed was missing from his house.

Why Italian royalty had been called to Chicago for a meeting of all the bosses was beyond me. The New York Mafia shouldn't have warranted such drastic measures.

A door opened, and a few seconds later, Sofia came in, flashing me a brilliant smile. "She's good and asking for you, Nic."

I hesitated for a second, divided in mind. Getting back to Mia's side was my priority, but this discussion wasn't finished. "Why?"

Stefano answered after pulling El into his lap. "The Verretti family wants in."

Goddammit. "They're not based in Chicago." *They had better not try to make the Five Families six.* To do that, they would have to move to our city.

"Extenuating circumstances, and it may not come to that," Stefano explained. "They want to be our allies, and it makes sense."

That was all I needed to hear. I pushed off the bar and headed toward the door, needing to see Mia. Marco stood and stopped me at the doorway. I spoke before he could. "I don't trust him."

"I know." Marco sighed. "None of us missed the times he's left to conduct business out of earshot. We'll get to the bottom of this before any final decisions are made."

With a clipped nod, I acknowledged what he was saying. "He's been very focused on Mia."

Marco ran a hand through his hair. "He mentioned that he didn't know about some of the things she'd endured. Not only that, but he called Stefano when she was missing. He was worried, and he demanded that the Five Families get involved in finding her and specifically not return her to Joey Tucci."

Interesting. I hadn't known that, and it changed things. "He's still keeping something from us."

"I agree." He clapped me on the back. "We'll get it figured out. Go see Mia and find out when we can travel with them."

When I entered the temporary post-op room, it was to find Mia sitting up in an oversized chair with her leg bandaged and propped on an ottoman, an IV with a new bag of fluids hooked to her and a fleece blanket tucked under her arms. Her mom's gold necklace was pooled in her lap.

I pulled a chair next to hers and took her hand in mine, running my thumb back and forth over her soft skin. "How are you feeling?" She looked tired, but some color had returned to her cheeks.

"Better. They're both dead."

I studied her, searching for any signs of emotional trauma or pain. She was pale but already looking better out of the bloody and wet clothes. "They are. Guido bled out from the artery you hit when you shot him. And I took care of Ricco."

She nodded once. "Good. I wanted to make sure." A second passed before she glanced at her necklace. "It got damaged."

I knew how much it meant to her and picked it up to inspect the bottom of the bar near where the flower was engraved. "We'll get it fixed."

"No. I mean yes, but not until after." She pulled her hand from mine then pointed to the small separation of what looked almost like a gold stopper at the bottom of the bar. "I couldn't pull it out, but I think my mom wanted me to open it because of the flower. I don't know. Everything else that had one of the flowers I associated with her has led to a secret she wanted me to know about."

I pinched the tiny bit of gold between my fingers and wiggled it back and forth until it came loose. A rolled piece of paper was fitted into the hollowed-out portion of the bar. That, too, came out, and I unrolled the note, which was no bigger than the size of an insert from a fortune cookie. I held the paper so she could read it first.

After she did, her purplish-blue eyes jumped to mine, and the small amount of color she'd regained drained from her cheeks. "Oh my God."

Alarmed, I flipped the note back so that I could read it. In what I assumed to be her mother's flowy script, there was confirmation of who she'd had an affair with. It wasn't new information, but what it revealed changed everything.

Joey Tucci wasn't Mia's biological father. Arturo Verretti was, and Dante, Cal, and Adriano were her half brothers.

CHAPTER TWENTY-FIVE

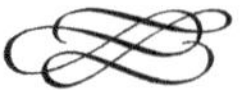

MIA

The slow, steady drip of the IV contrasted with the thundering of my pulse. I should have been calm, happy. What I'd learned was good, certainly better than being a spawn of the devil himself. But I didn't know what to feel. Too many emotions surrounded Mom's note, and I clung to Nico's hand as more pieces of my life fell into place.

Joey Tucci was not my father.

The completely messed-up part was that I didn't think he was entirely sure I was his blood in the first place. But doing a paternity test would have driven home how the wife he'd supposedly worshipped had betrayed him for far longer than he'd thought.

He was a psychopath. He'd sentenced me to death by Ricco's hand without certainty that I wasn't his daughter. A shiver danced over me at how history had almost repeated itself, at least by the family line that had dealt a death blow to my mother.

The slow back and forth of Nico's thumb over my hand kept me tethered to him, to the life I had chosen, the only reality that mattered.

"This changes things." Nico's deep voice pulled me away from my thoughts.

I tightly clutched his hand. "I guess it does." He'd done so much for me already. I didn't want to rock the boat. "We can wait. I know you're not sure about Dante, and I don't want to put you in a position where you have to deal with them because of me."

"No. That's not what I meant." He cupped my face, the pad of his thumb caressing my cheek, and I leaned into his touch.

"We'll tell everyone now, and Trey can get the testing started to prove they're your half brothers. It'll sever any ties that Joey thinks he has to you. And with Ricco dead, he'll want to use you in any way he can."

"But he ordered Ricco to kill me." I frowned, reeling that he could think he had any rights where I was concerned. "I think it's fair to say he's washed his hands of me."

"Not after I killed Ricco."

The full impact of the blow Nico had delivered to Joey settled around me. Ricco had become an integral part of the business, and Joey relied heavily on him.

"Joey doesn't have anyone else to help him with the family." Nico echoed my thoughts. "He may have cut his losses where you were concerned then let his temper and the past influence his decision. Once he learns about Ricco and how the loss will affect his business, that'll change. You'll be seen once more as a pawn for power. He'll be desperate."

"Okay." My stomach was a jumble of nerves. I was glad I wasn't recovering in the same room as Tony. He was still unconscious. The last thing he needed was to be disturbed, and I needed these private moments with Nico. "Let's tell them now." I was drowsy and needed to do it before I napped, preferably in Nico's arms and on the jet home.

"We need to speak to Stefano and Marco first." He leaned down and pressed a quick kiss to my lips, leaving me wanting more before releasing my hand and going into the other room. I rested my head against the back of the chair, a dull ache the only discomfort from the gunshot wound, thanks to whatever Trey had fed into my IV.

I snuggled under the warm blanket, fighting the urge to doze. The click of the door opening sent a tiny jolt of adrenaline through me, enough to pop my eyelids open, and I waited to say anything until Nico, Stefano, and Marco were inside and the door was closed.

"How are you feeling?" Marco took a chair on the other side of mine, opposite where Nico sat. The two brothers looked so different. Marco's coloring was closer to mine with black hair but green eyes instead of my strange purplish ones. Nico, Trey, and Sofia all had dark-brown hair and whiskey-colored eyes. The similarities between the siblings were in their model-worthy features—Sofia's classic bone structure and chiseled... everything... for the guys. Their mom had been a supermodel, and I could see it in them.

Marco grinned, and I snapped back to his question about how I was doing. "I'm good. Tired." I shifted my shoulder, trying to get comfortable. "And sore."

Stefano remained standing with his arms crossed over his chest. He did give me a small smile, which eased his predatory presence from freeze-in-our-tracks to merely powerful like the other men in the Five Families.

"We discovered some interesting news." Nico picked up the tiny piece of paper that curled at the ends, wanting to return to its prior rolled status. "Mia's father isn't Joey Tucci."

Marco took the paper from Nico, and Stefano moved closer so he could read the handwritten words over his shoulder. "Well, isn't that interesting." Marco chuckled.

"We couldn't have asked for a better scenario," Stefano said. "We need to put it to a vote between all the bosses, but I suggest we ally with the Verrettis and make them the spokesperson for the New York syndicate."

"Dante's hiding something." Nico's voice cracked like a whip, his mistrust in the idea of bringing them in loud and clear.

I wanted to protest. I got why Nico felt the way he did. We knew Guido had set the bomb, and Dante was being cagey about something. But I knew him. It wasn't anything against the Five Families. His issues were with New York.

"That may be," Marco responded, "and we'll find out what it is. What's important to this decision is how Dante and his brothers have been invested in Mia's safety from the start. They've shared intel they had on the Tucci and Amato families and joined forces with us to destroy the sex-trafficking business Joey's been relying on to grow his wealth."

"We'll discuss this at home," Stefano commanded before his gaze fell to me, his voice softening. "Trey will take a swab for a sibling DNA test after you break the news to the Verretti brothers."

I could only nod, my throat too tight for words to slip through. I'd never expected to be able to shed one horrible family and gain not one but two who wanted to protect and care for me. The way Nico and the Chicago Mafia had embraced me into the fold was nothing short of a miracle. Would the Verrettis do the same? A cauldron of nervous excitement churned in my gut when Nico went to the other room, only to return with everyone, not just Dante, Cal, and Adriano.

Sofia, Emiliana, and El pushed through the group of guys. Nico shoved Sofia over and resumed his place by my side, and she snorted. But Enzo just tugged her into him, laughing at how she rolled her eyes. Emiliana peeked at my bandage, and Trey moved forward and smacked her hand. Stefano growled and crowded in too. I couldn't help but laugh. They cared. I hadn't had that since Mom was alive.

"You okay with that little scratch you got?" Sofia winked and then giggled when Nico glared.

"How was it when Enz was shot, Sof?" Nico frowned.

She winced, the color draining from her face. Enzo wrapped his arms around her waist, pressing a kiss to her neck. "Sorry, Nic."

Nico grunted then locked his gaze on Dante. That was my cue. Marco and Stefano moved enough away, so I had a clear view of them. I took a deep breath then ripped off the metaphorical Band-Aid.

I lifted the necklace to show them. "This was damaged during the mess with Ricco and Guido, which turned out to be a good thing, since Mom left me a note rolled up inside it."

Something flashed in Dante's silvery gaze. Did he know?

"Joey isn't my father." I handed the note to Nico, and he passed it to Dante. "My father was Arturo Verretti."

Adriano laughed. "Thank fuck."

Cal smacked his brother on the head before grinning at me. "We suspected but weren't sure."

Dante moved forward then pressed a kiss to my forehead. He winked as he said, "Welcome to the family, little sis."

CHAPTER TWENTY-SIX

NICO

On crutches, Mia stood next to me inside the Chicago warehouse where we held important meetings. The only key people missing were all the other Mafia women, as the meeting was between bosses and underbosses. Max and Luc had been taxed with meeting the Sicilian royalty at the airport. Mia's presence was an exception because of Joey Tucci and the Verrettis, who would arrive soon.

Mia rested one of the crutches against the table then leaned into me, and I inhaled the scent of cinnamon-spiced vanilla from her hair as I wrapped my arm around her waist and drew her close. It was chilly indoors, as if the bitter January wind had found a way inside. No windows were on the first floor. The upper level that was mostly open made it harder to keep the heat on the first floor—but it wasn't meant to be comfortable.

At times, we took enemies there to torture information from them. Meetings held on the premises weren't always friendly. The walls were steel, and there was a large table where we could gather for the commission if everyone chose to sit.

Four days had passed since we'd been in New York, and she'd shared the news from her mom's note with the Verretti brothers. They were due to arrive with the Tucci and Amato bosses. Before they did, we would have a few minutes alone with the Sicilians we were descended from. The New York Mafia didn't have the same ties. They originated in Italy but hadn't become Mafia until migrating to the States.

"Are you nervous?" I kept my voice low. Though we'd hosted several in recent years, the New York Mafia hadn't been invited to a commission in my lifetime. And what we were about to do would change that, at least with the Verretti family.

"Not about the commission." Mia tilted her head back and flashed me a small smile. "Only the confrontation that I want to have with Joey."

"If he missteps, he'll have several bullets in him." I wanted to be the one to put them there, although I knew everyone present would do the same.

"Hey, lovebirds." Enzo winked, strolling closer. "Ready for the show?"

Marco was talking with Stefano and snorted at Enzo's comment. "They are the show."

Stefano ran a hand through his closely cropped dark-blond hair then scowled as a ping sounded from his phone. "The Sicilians are almost here."

Five minutes later, the door opened, and a handful of older men in three-piece suits entered with Max and Luc. Their guards had been instructed to remain in their cars or outside, where ours patrolled.

Among the men were Vincenzo Brambilla, grandfather to Luc and Liliana, Mario Caruso, and Lorenzo Rossi. They were the oldest of the Italian royalty and who we'd dealt with a handful of times, such as when Stefano uncovered the rat in our families.

Vincenzo and Luc talked quietly and off to the side as the other men moved forward, their gaits slow, though none of them were to be underestimated.

"Gentlemen." Stefano's gruff voice filled the large room, bouncing off the polished cement floor. "We have news to share before the New York bosses arrive."

Since Mia was on my left side, I was free to reach for my gun in the shoulder holster if needed. I felt her fingers slide around the Glock tucked into the back of my waistband. While I was mostly sure how the meeting would unfold, bloodshed with so many powerful men present was likely.

Stefano and Max took turns filling them in on everything that had happened. Max had been elected to bring everyone up to speed because of his years living in Italy and his connection to Vincenzo. They briefed the Sicilians about the Tucci trafficking ring that we'd blown wide open, Joey's early ties to Ivan Pavlov, and what led to the death of both Ricco and Guido. They brought everyone up to speed about past trouble with Guido Amato stalking Summer and his bid for power with his plan to kill his father, something that hadn't come to pass. And finally, they shared that the results from the expedited sibling DNA test proved that Dante, Cal, and Adriano were Mia's brothers.

"I look forward to filling your parents in on all the happenings while they're enjoying retirement in Italy." Vincenzo chuckled, his eyes crinkling at the corners as he fixed his gaze on me. "Now, is this why you brought us here?"

"Eager to get back to Catherine?" I teased. Trey knew what he was doing when he sent Catherine, a dear friend of our family and Mom's former makeup artist, to stay with him recently while undergoing medical treatment. Given the way his face lit up, it had been good for both of them.

"I am."

Mario and Lorenzo grunted, but it was Mario who spoke. "Let's get whatever you've concocted over with so we can return."

The door crashed open, and Mia tensed against me as Dante,

Cal, and Adriano Verretti entered with Leo Amato and Joey Tucci on their heels—the main reason we were gathered. There would be no denying orders with everyone present. While we didn't need such a grand gesture, the Verretti brothers would initially keep the Tucci and Amato families in line.

Leo Amato looked resigned. After all he'd gone through with his son. It could have gone one of two ways. What he exhibited was the better side of the coin.

Mia dropped her arm from my waist and put an inch of space between us. I didn't like it but respected her for wanting to stand against Joey on her own, although she would never be alone again.

"Why is she here?" Joey zeroed in on Mia, the only woman present.

She raised her chin, her midnight hair rippling over her back, and smirked. Her gaze dropped to his gauze-wrapped hand. "To make sure you receive the report with all the bosses present."

Stefano slammed his palm down on the table, a copy of the DNA results beneath his hand. He pushed it down the table and crossed his arms over his chest. "You have no claim to Mia La Rosa by blood—you are not her father."

Joey cast his gaze to the papers as red infused his face. His hand clenched into a fist at his side. The one I'd put a bullet into remained limp. "This is fake."

"It isn't." Dante stepped close, crowding Joey. "My brothers and I participated in the DNA test with Mia. She is our sister and under our protection."

I cleared my throat, amused.

Dante paused then notched his head in my direction. "As well as her husband's."

Mia grabbed her other crutch and limped toward Joey, and I took position at her back, my body tensing to strike should he make even the slightest move toward her.

"I'm no longer yours to control, bend to your will, or use as a pawn to gain power." Mia's words were soft but weighty. There was steel beneath them and in her hardened stare and confident posture.

Joey chuckled, his fist uncurling as a cruel twist slashed across his mouth. "Little girl, that's where you're wrong." He took a step forward.

The Verretti brothers bristled, and I shifted so that I was next to Mia, flicking my wrist so that the knife strapped to my forearm dropped into my hand. I held it at my side for the time being.

"This marriage between you and Nico wasn't authorized. You went against my plans, and if it's to stand, I'm owed compensation by the La Rosa family."

"You're owed nothing." Her voice was firm. "But I am. You've told me about your actions toward Mom. It doesn't make sense. You should have been lenient—you worshipped her, at least from what you've told me."

"Betrayal is just that, Mia—betrayal. She had to be punished. And the only proper punishment was death."

Mia shook her head, disgust clear on her face. "No matter how many times you've explained it, I can't rationalize your actions from someone who supposedly loved my mom. And to give Ricco orders to kill me? It's clear you care for no one."

"Betrayal isn't forgivable. Once done to me, you become nothing."

"And you are nothing to me."

Joey's perilous control snapped, and he lunged. His uninjured hand extended, fingers about to wrap around her throat. I whipped my arm up and pressed the blade against his carotid artery, freezing him before he could touch her delicate skin.

I held him there, and Mia's laughter filled the room. "You're outmatched. Not only that, but you have no control here." Her gaze jumped to Stefano. "Even less than you thought."

"To answer your question about why we called a commission, Vincenzo," Stefano addressed the roomful of tense and amused expressions within the warehouse. "Due to the joining of the La Rosa and Verretti families through Nico and Mia's marriage, the Five Families have decided on an alliance. In addition, Dante Verretti will be the spokesperson for the New York syndicate."

A growl sounded from Joey, and I pressed the blade hard enough to create a shallow cut. Blood trickled over the metal. "Careful, Joey." I eased closer, begging him to press his luck. "Stefano is your boss. And now, so is Dante."

Joey flung himself backward, a growl ripping from his throat before he stormed from the building. I moved to follow, eager to end his miserable life. Mia wrapped a hand around my bicep, and she leaned into me, halting my momentum.

"Let him go. He's nothing to us."

I lowered the knife and drew her into my arms, slanting my mouth over hers, unable to resist her. The kiss was brief, not what I wanted it to be, but it was not the place to lower my guard. It would only put Mia at risk, and I never wanted that, regardless of how selfish I wanted to be by losing myself in her.

"Let's make this official," Alfonso Caruso said, "and put the Verretti family hierarchy in New York to a vote."

Stefano started the vote, and each boss followed. When it was done, Dante and his brothers mingled with the Sicilians as Vincenzo moved from his grandson's side, which enabled Luc to speak to the Verretti brothers—he and Max hadn't been in New York with us.

"When is the honeymoon?" Vincenzo bent over Mia's hand and pressed a kiss onto its back. "And it had better be in Italy."

She blushed, and my heart swelled at the sight. "We'll see you in a few weeks." When she turned to me, her eyes shining with happiness, I wanted to give her the world—and I would.

CHAPTER TWENTY-SEVEN

MIA

Two weeks later...

Nico threaded his fingers with mine as we walked along the shore. The waves crashed against the densely packed sand with a soothing, rhythmic back and forth. My leg had healed enough for just a light bandage—the skin glue did its job—and I'd ditched the crutches. We were in jeans and light sweaters, as it wasn't overly warm in Mondella, Italy in January. Nico's sister had graciously offered her and Enzo's home when we'd mentioned it was where we wanted to go, and upon arrival the day before, I'd immediately fallen in love with it.

We had six days left, and I wanted to enjoy every moment of it because being there with Nico was pure heaven, especially given everything we'd been through. After the commission, things had settled down enough so that we could take a honeymoon, which was still surreal to me.

Thanks to Nico and his siblings—the Five Families, really—Joey no longer had a hold over my life. Not only that, but he was struggling to recover from the immediate and final shutdown of his trafficking ring. It was a sore spot with all the Italians in Chicago and Sicily because of what had happened to Emiliana. The Five Families and Sicilians had decreed that the Tucci line would be demolished if there was even a hint of Joey dabbling in sex trafficking. Their executioner would be the Verretti family.

Since the commission, I'd spoken with Dante, Cal, and Adriano several times. We'd always gotten along, but the knowledge that we were related had brought us even closer, giving me the sense of family I'd always craved. As the girl who always had been an afterthought or forgotten once Mom died, it was incredible to feel wanted by them, Nico, and the Chicago Mafia. And Sofia and all the other Mafia wives had welcomed me into their tight-knit group. I'd never imagined my life like this, and I wouldn't take it for granted.

"What are you thinking?" Nico tugged me closer, away from the water's foam that rolled precariously close to my feet.

I released his hand and wrapped my arm around his waist, leaning into him. "Just how something terrible ended up giving me you."

"Hmm." He bent and pressed a kiss to my lips. "You think you're the lucky one?"

"I know I am." The wind picked up, and I shivered, burrowing closer.

He turned us back toward the house. "What do you think about it here?"

"What's not to love?" I scanned the tourist-free coastal town with its pristine, very private beach then up the steps, not far from where we walked to the oceanfront villa.

"My sister urged me to purchase property here even if I wasn't ready to build." He pointed to about a mile down. "That's ours. We can build a house whenever you want."

I stopped, forcing him to as well. "You're serious?" *Could we have our own sanctuary here to get away whenever possible?*

Nico grinned, and the sexy dimple on his left cheek deepened. My fingers curled at his waist from the need to touch him.

"I'll take that as a yes." He chuckled, urging my feet to move again, and we angled toward the stairs that led to Sofia and Enzo's place.

When we reached the stairs, we climbed them quickly, passing by the infinity-edge pool and hot tub. Last night, we'd gone in, and I wanted to do so again. Nico opened the screen door to the lanai, where ceiling fans swirled in a slow paddle above our heads as we crossed to the sliding doors. I loved how they had two entrances to the back, one with a lanai and the other a large glass slider that disappeared into the wall to offer the option of indoor-outdoor living.

His hand dipped under the back of my sweater, and my body heated at the simple touch as he ushered me in ahead of him. I gave him a hooded glance over my shoulder, telegraphing what I wanted.

Desire flared on his chiseled features, and my body responded with a surge of need. His hands latched onto my hips, and I shivered at the promise in his eyes as he guided me to the room where we were staying. Then all thoughts fled when he eased my sweater over my head, his fingers trailing in the wake of the thin cashmere, and my stomach clenched. His shirt followed mine to the floor.

Needing to touch him, too, I buried my fingers in his hair, rising on my toes to tug him closer, then brushed my lips over his in a slow caress. His deep growl sent shivers over my exposed skin, and I pressed against his warm chest as he teased my mouth open. I was barely aware of my clothes melting away as he explored my mouth. Heat radiated from his body, even more so with all our clothes gone.

He turned my body so that he was at the edge of the bed and

then trailed kisses along my neck, his teeth scraping my hyper-sensitive skin. My pulse fluttered beneath his lips, and I ran my hands along his shoulders, reveling in the way his muscles bunched and flexed beneath the pads of my fingers.

When he slid his hands around my hips and lifted, I complied and wrapped my legs around his waist, clinging to his shoulders. He carried me as if I weighed nothing then settled his back to the headboard, and I straddled him. His hard length pressed at the apex of my thighs, and I moaned, needing more.

His hands explored my body, cupping my breast and rolling a nipple between his fingers, and I arched into his hand. Then the pad of his thumb found my clit, massaging in slow, tantalizing circles. Heat pooled, and I squirmed against him, craving friction, needing him to fill me. I trailed my hand over the hard ridges of his abdomen then gripped his hard length and gently squeezed, tearing a guttural moan from him. Power surged through me, and I lined him up against my entrance. His hand found my hip, the other spreading the slick wetness of my desire over the sensitive bundle of nerves, causing me to lose all sense of control I'd thought I had.

I sank lower, reveling in how my body stretched and squeezed him and in how it felt so incredibly full. Rocking my hips, I set a slow, sensual rhythm, my breath coming faster. I arched into him as he pressed against my core. He gripped my hips with both hands, increasing the rhythm, each thrust more powerful than the last. Pressure built in me, and I clung to him, urging him to go faster, harder. I would never get enough of him or what he did to me.

My body shook with need as I balanced precariously on the edge, desperate to fall over into bliss. "Nico, please." I didn't recognize my breathy voice, my body shaking with need. Perspiration beaded along my hairline, and waves of ecstasy flooded every hypersensitive nerve ending in my body as he masterfully played my body like a fine instrument.

"You drive me crazy, Mia." His deep voice rasped against my heated skin. "I'm never letting you go."

His words struck a chord deep inside me, and my head fell back as stars burst behind my eyelids in cresting waves. His movements increased as he chased my climax with his own.

My body was limp, spent, and exhausted as he trailed unhurried kisses along my neck. A whimper escaped my lips as he withdrew from inside, and I missed the fullness immediately.

He lifted me, pulled back the covers, then lay me on the mattress before climbing in beside me, pulling me to him so that my head rested on his shoulder, and I tangled my legs with his. I never thought I would have such a connection to a man, and I was never letting Nico go.

He pulled the sheet and duvet over us, and I snuggled closer. His fingers trailed circles along my arm as our heartbeats regulated and slowed.

"I think I knew you could be the one the moment I turned around to find you standing there on the beach, aiming a gun at my chest." Nico broke the easy silence between us. "There was this connection—it's hard to explain, but it grew stronger with each day we spent together."

I tilted my head back to see his expression then smiled. "I know what you mean. I felt it too." It was different, nothing I'd ever experienced before. Special.

"Our life won't be easy. But it'll be full of passion. And Mia" —he brushed a few strands of my hair from my cheek—"know that I'll fight for you until the bitter end."

I couldn't stop the tears from welling in my eyes. For a girl who'd never meant more than a means to an end, a bargaining chip for power once my mom had died, what he said meant more to me than he could ever know. With that passionate statement, he'd told me I was worth fighting for, that I mattered. "Thank you."

Nico leaned in and kissed my temple, whispering against my heated skin, "I love you, Mia."

I moaned at the sweetness of how he touched me, physically and emotionally. "I love you too." When my head stopped spinning from how he made me feel, I finished what I wanted to say. "And thank you for taking a chance and agreeing to marry me."

In a low growl, he said, "It was easily the best decision I ever made." Then he grazed his lips over mine until I opened for him. I knew then that I wouldn't have changed a single second of my life, as it had brought me to this very moment.

The End

Be sure to check out any of the other series or single titles. For more Mafia romance, BORROWED TIME (Verretti Crime Family, book 1) will be coming soon.

Subscribe to Amy's newsletter for the latest releases and news: https://bit.ly/3CGcdSF

If you enjoyed reading RIVALS as much as I did writing it, I hope you'll consider leaving a review.

ACKNOWLEDGMENTS

Ahh—this series! Just so much fun. And Rivals, well, it's bittersweet as it's the last. There will be a few short stories, and the Five Families will reappear in the Verretti Crime Family spin-off series. We don't have to say goodbye to them. Trust me. I'm not ready for that. And if you're curious about how the series began, Defiant Princess will give you a glimpse into that. I'm hoping to get that to you soon. If you're not already on it, join my newsletter for updates on releases and news.

I am beyond grateful for my family's support and encouragement. They are truly amazing

My critique partners have been with me through the entire Mafia Elite journey, and I value their creative input: Emily Albright, Kristin Kisska, and Candace Irvin. I'm thankful to have them in my inner circle.

I have an incredible team of editors. Taylor Anhalt always has a significant role in the development of my books. I loved her content edit and how she helped shape this story into what it is today. I have a fabulous team from Red Adept Editing. Kate Birdsall and Taylor Anhalt, and I'm so lucky to be working with them both. They help to make my stories better

T.E. Black Designs, who did the cover design, is a dream to work with. No matter the genre, she understands my vision and can match that with the genre's vibe. As always, each project exceeds my expectations.

I'm grateful to have Colleen Noyes with Itsy Bitsy Book Bits and Danielle Sanchez with Wildfire Marketing Solutions in my corner, working their magic to make each release successful.

Last but certainly not least, a special thank you to all the bloggers and readers who have encouraged and helped me along the way and continue to make my dream a reality.

Thank you.

ABOUT THE AUTHOR

Amy McKinley is the *USA Today* best-selling author of the romantic suspense thriller Gray Ghost Novels, Deadly Isles Special Ops, Covert Recruits, Mafia Elite, Verretti Crime Family, Moonlit Destination Series, the Five Fates paranormal romance books, and several standalone titles. Her edge-of-your-seat books are filled with surprising twists and just the right amount of heat and danger. She lives in Illinois with her husband, two daughters, two sons, and three mischievous cats.

You can find her at:
www.AmyMcKinley.com

Subscribe to Amy's newsletter for cover reveals, book announcements, and giveaways: https://bit.ly/3CGcdSF

goodreads.com/amymckinley_author
bookbub.com/authors/amy-mckinley
facebook.com/amymckinleyauthor
instagram.com/amymckinleyauthor

Borrowed Time

My Enemy's Bed

Fractured Lies

\-

Covert Recruits (coming soon)

Irina

Sasha

Zena

Nadia

Katya

\-

Standalone Titles

Shattered Melody

Siren's Call: Cursed Seas

Fake Fiancé (A Second Chance Office Romance)

\-

Moonlit Destination Series

Moonlit Whisper

Moonlit Kiss

Moonlit Mirage

Five Fates Series

Hidden

Taken